Lady Wood

Seadrift

A novel. Vol. 2

Lady Wood

Seadrift
A novel. Vol. 2

ISBN/EAN: 9783337213572

Printed in Europe, USA, Canada, Australia, Japan

Cover: Foto ©Andreas Hilbeck / pixelio.de

More available books at **www.hansebooks.com**

SEADRIFT.

A Novel.

BY

LADY WOOD,

AUTHOR OF 'ROSEWARN,' 'SABINA,' 'ON CREDIT,' ETC.

IN THREE VOLUMES.

VOL. II.

LONDON:

CHAPMAN AND HALL, 193 PICCADILLY.

1871.

SEADRIFT.

CHAPTER I.

'Excuse me, then ; you know my heart ;
   But dearest friends, alas, must part.' GAY.

IN the mean time Martha and Philip strolled through the lanes between the gardens and the lake, and Philip talked eagerly whilst Martha listened with more of pleasure than she had felt since the arrival of the letter from Norfolk, which had broken up their chance of domestic association. Yet Philip spoke of separation for more than a year; not much more perhaps, but quite a year.

What was there in this information that conveyed any comfort to Martha's mind? Simply that the beautiful subject of the portrait Philip had copied would be farther removed from the possibility of being seen by him. It was not quite easy for Martha to understand all that Philip meant to convey, but she gathered thus much.

In the first place, Lord Tynedale had given him ten guineas more for his copy of his grand-niece, as she was called, and had expressed himself so well pleased with the performance, that he had proposed to Philip to reside in Rome for the next twelve months, to copy several pictures for his lordship, which he required to cover the walls of a room in Tynedale Park. His lordship did not state, that he had quarrelled already with two painters whom he had employed in this occupation, because he had interfered so pertinaciously with their work, from the conviction that he knew better than they did how it ought to be executed.

This, however, could not affect Philip, as on this occasion his lordship was to remain in England, and could scarcely send his criticisms across the seas on copies he had never seen, to interfere with the execution of the order he had given. Philip was to receive three hundred pounds for the year, and at the same rate so long as he remained at Rome. This was to include travelling expenses. For this sum he would have to supply himself with an English master, and make as many copies of the pictures specified by his lordship as his industry permitted. When these had been completed, Mr. Rose was to return to England, nominally to assist in placing them; really that, with his art perfected by study, and by the experience gained by copying the finest works of art in the world, he might be fitted to immortalise the person of Lord Tynedale on canvas.

Poor Philip knew not the honour intended him. Could he have been aware of the sufferings of previous artists when employed on this work, he might have shrunk from the engagement which entailed such a termination. Lord Tynedale was handsome, and had he been content with a true representation, the portraits of him could scarcely have failed to make good pictures. But he could not forget the youthful face which had beamed on him from the mirror so many, years ago.

Could he have been contented to trust the representation of himself to the pencil of an experienced painter, he might have obtained a favourable likeness; but he insisted on having no marks of age.

'D—n it! take away that frightful line running from the nostril to the corner of the mouth! I am sure you have marked the crow's-feet unnecessarily! Darken the eyebrows.' And taking the brush from the unwilling hand of the painter, my lord touched up the face according to his own idea; and having put all likeness utterly to rout, he returned the brush to the fingers of the unhappy artist, with this assertion and injunction: 'Now I have given you a notion how it ought to be; soften it down and finish it up.'

Sometimes the painter tried to please Lord Tynedale by obliterating from his representation all traces of age, and taking forty years from his life. Then his lordship's pale face glowed with nascent satisfaction; which went on increasing as the artist transferred to the canvas the fleeting bloom of age, which was here made to represent the rich glow on the cheek of adolescence. The delighted peer saw himself as he believed himself to be, certainly as he used to be. His happiness lasted till some spectator came into the room, and dispelled the illusion, if a person in an inferior rank, in some words like these: 'O, 'tis very well, but does not do your lordship justice;' a safe generality under which the critic may escape giving a reason for the judgment pronounced. Sometimes, if the easel and materials for painting were not in the way, to point out the subject of the portrait, it was simply not recognised; a heart-breaking situation for the man who had spent time, unwearied patience, and exhausted sight, in trying to follow the erratic fancies of the great sitter.

Alas, unconscious of their doom, the little victims play—*i. e.* Philip and Martha rejoiced. Martha made Philip repeat the intelligence over and over again. That he was to receive three hundred a year for his labour in the field of art seemed to her too good to be true; in fact, utterly incredible. It was more than Dr. Mereside had, or the clergyman, and two-thirds more than the sum subscribed to pay the Dissenting minister; but Philip assured her, that the doctor himself had made it perfectly clear to him in Latin, and Lord Tynedale as precisely as he could in English. The doctor, too, was going to write to an English family living in the Piazza di Spagna, with whom he resided when he had been at Rome, and with whom he recommended Philip to make arrangements to board and lodge him.

Before all these details had been conveyed by Philip's broken English to the ear of Martha, he had shown her the gold he had received for the copy of the picture; and eager to give Martha and her mother a remembrance of him, he ha turned back to the jeweller's shop, and purchased a ring for his betrothed, and a silver nutmeg-grater for Mrs. Clemens.

No wonder that the two prolonged their walk through the tamarisk lanes that skirted the lake on one side, and the sloping gardens on the other. There was small beauty in the wintry landscape, but contentment in Philip's heart, and contentment, mixed with a perplexing tumult, in that of Martha. She longed to marry him at once, that she might make the tie which united them eternal, at least in this world; but this she could scarcely propose, while Philip did not seem to have an idea on the subject. He was very sweet and tender in his manner; but his feeling was like that of an eager boy, whose mother detains him with cautions and caresses, while he longs to break away from her in some eager chase for amusement, and kisses her a bribe that he may depart the sooner.

Mrs. Clemens was very proud of her silver nutmeg-grater, and in the course of the next day she boiled some groats, and carried the gruel in a jug to the lying-in wife of a fisherman; nice and hot, she said, with just a drop of her husband's old brandy in it, and added a flavour of nutmeg by the bedside, managing that the light should strike on the polished silver when the eyes of the patient and of the nurse were fixed on it. She knew that the first neighbour who came in would hear of it, and that the fame thereof would travel over Seadrift before twenty-four hours had elapsed. The gift of the handsome young man who was making such heaps of money, and who was engaged to Martha Clemens!

Indeed, so entirely was Mrs. Clemens occupied by this new possession, that she was constantly taking it out of her pocket to polish it with her handkerchief; and fearful lest her keys and thimble should scratch it, she retired to her room, out of the way of Martha's sneering criticisms on her sewing, and straightway constructed a little pocket within the large one, in which the nutmeg-grater might rest securely, and far removed from friction and undue pressure.

She did not lose much conversation by her absence. Martha was sulky with her, because she thought that her mother, instead of being so childishly pleased with such a toy, should have driven her own thoughts in a groove similar to that of Martha's anent the desirability of Philip's marrying her at once; then Martha thought she might join him when Mrs. Clemens was settled at Lynn.

On three hundred a year surely they might both live in luxury at Rome. Why did not her mother suggest this? 'Surely,' Martha said to herself, 'any person but one so unspeakably silly would have thought of it. But my mother never had any sense!' Had Philip determined not to marry Martha before he went to Italy, he could not have hit upon a better expedient than the little gift he had made to his future mother-in-law, which engrossed all her thoughts, to the exclusion even of Martha's interests.

Had she thought of their immediate marriage, it is unlikely she would have encouraged the idea. She could not leave a dying sister, who entreated for her society; and she would not for an instant have consented to Martha's leaving *her*, as Philip would have had a right to demand, should she have become his wife. Even could she have become reconciled to the separation, if he remained in England, the circumstance of his going to live in a country where all the inhabitants were Catholics, and at Rome especially, where the Scarlet Lady of Babylon reigned supreme, would have filled her simple Methodistical mind with the greatest horror. So Martha had no remedy. She became sad, when the first flush of the good news for Philip had subsided, and asked when he would have to go. She had a vague notion that it would not be till after they had departed for Lynn.

Philip could give them no information. It would, he thought, depend on the doctor; but it was a point which, with his imperfect knowledge of English, he had understood but vaguely.

Martha set to work that evening to repair his scanty wardrobe and economise his money for him, as only an able woman can. She begged of her mother one of the smallest of her brothers' boxes for his use, and collected together everything he was likely to want, even threaded needles, scissors, buttons, tapes, and thread. His socks were mended with the most elaborate neatness, by taking up every alternate thread. It was not an unusual exhibition of skill, resulting from love; for Martha would have considered herself disgraced by mending them in any other manner.

She was very silent as she worked; whilst Philip sang so cheerfully, that Mrs. Clemens asked Martha, with wonder in her tone, whether she thought Mr. Rose could have heard the monks sing such merry tunes in the monastery where he was brought up.

With some trouble Martha explained to him

her mother's question; and he admitted that what he sang was not chants or canticles, but the lays of the mulcteers as they wound round the hill-side, sometimes seen between the groves of chest-nut- and cork-trees, but more frequently heard in rich sonorous melodies, which died away on the passing breeze.

Mrs. Clemens was satisfied with this explanation. She did not mind hearing what the drovers sang, poor fellows; but she could not abide the thought of them Papist hymns.

Philip looked up roguishly, and began a Latin chant; on which the old lady stopped her ears, and threatened to go out of the room.

His former life seemed very different from that in which his present hours were passed; but hope had gilded each portion of his career—the hope of success in his art, which now seemed verging towards fruition.

Philip had never forgotten those old gray arches of his first recollections, the long vistas of the solemn cloisters, and the pealing hymn which had awakened their echoes. He had never heard the truth of the Catholic religion disputed. He was a true son of the Church, obedient and un-doubting. His heart often turned with yearning affection to the recollection of those venerable men who had sustained his tottering steps in infancy, glad of a subject on which to lavish their unused tenderness, who had guided his footsteps aright, and taught him to practise morality, and worship purity and truth. They had taught him, also, that the talent he possessed had been bestowed by Heaven for the glory of God and of the blessed Virgin; and that in the career he should run in the world, every other feeling should be subservient to that great end.

To do them justice, they had never urged his taking the vows. He had been a waif and a stray thrown on their protection, and they seem to have felt towards him as parents who, having practised stern self-denial all their lives, shrink from inflicting it on their offspring. He might return to them again, if, battered with the storms of fate, he should once more require an asylum. But they looked forward to his making a name in the world, and acquiring wealth; under which circumstances he would doubtless remember the holy saint whose votaries had protected his childhood.

CHAPTER II.

'Abruptness is an eloquence in parting, when spinning-out
the time is but the weaving of new sorrow.'
SIR JOHN SUCKLING.

IT was well that Martha had been so active
for Philip's comfort. On the following morning
Dr. Mereside came, and stated that he was to
proceed to Plymouth that night, for the purpose
of embarking for Italy, in a vessel about to sail
immediately.

The worthy doctor had rather expedited the
departure, which was a great relief to his mind
on personal considerations; it saved him from the
direful wrath of Mrs. Mereside, when she should
have found that Philip was to be quartered on
her for a month, or even for an indefinite period;
for how to get rid of a homeless guest is a question
which has troubled many hosts, and will probably
continue to do so to the end of time.

'Never,' that sagacious lady would say—'never
receive a guest whose uplifted foot is unconscious
where in the world it may next be placed. Never
take in a young person who wants a situation, and

who will never find one so long as her do-nothing
state in your home suits her. Never take in a
lady and her daughter, however intellectual the
mother and charming the daughter, who have let
their house, and taken a smaller one which is not
quite ready for them. The intellect of the one
and the charms of the other will only serve, like
the legs of the octopos, to embrace you more
closely and strangle you more effectually. Did not
Mrs. Bolitho tell me,' continued the doctor's wife,
warming with her subject, ' that James the valet
had mentioned a picture hanging at Tynedale of
a young lady, about twenty-eight or thirty years
of age, very handsome, and with a look of strong
determination in her face, in the dress of Queen
Anne's time, of whom all that is known is, that
she rode over with some friends to call at Tynedale, and decided to remain to dine, when the rest
of the party refused? What was the consequence?
She never left Tynedale for two-and-twenty years!
With what marvellous arts she must have made
good her holding! This must have been the result of inviting a woman without a home. These
home-seekers have generally some means of making themselves agreeable to the influential member
of the family, and make a party against the legiti-

mate lord or lady, whoever may be the hitherto
vice-sovereign.'

This and much more had Mrs. Mereside frequently enumerated before her husband. He had
not forgotten it; and in the face of all her in-
junctions, he had asked a homeless man to stay
a month with him! Where was he to go at the
end of that time? Mrs. Mereside would feel that
he had brought to life a Frankenstein to pursue
him to the death, instead of a handsome young
Spaniard to paint his portrait.

So eager was the doctor to avoid the mental
'nips and bobs' which he expected from his wife,
that he determined to sacrifice the best part of
a couple of days, and two of the guineas he had
received for visits from Lord Tynedale, to take
Philip himself to Plymouth, and place him on
board the vessel. He liked the young man, and
had small confidence in his experience about travelling, besides that his imperfect knowledge of
English made it difficult for him to explain himself; moreover, he was certain to be at the mercy
of others, from his ignorance of the proper prices
of what he might require.

'I suppose Lord Tynedale pays your expenses,'
said the sharp lady.

'I certainly could not go, had he not given me the money,' said the doctor evasively; and Mrs. Mereside was satisfied.

There was another reason why Dr. Mereside wished to hurry Philip away. He knew that Martha Clemens was a very estimable young woman; but he knew also that a woman of twenty-seven was an unsuitable match for a youth of twenty. It was just seven years the wrong way; and though it must be owned that the majority of marriages which take place under such circumstances are not unhappy, the prejudice is against the union of two persons where the woman has numbered most winters.

He did not know they were engaged, for he knew how little the reports of Seadrift were to be credited, and the sooner he removed Philip from the temptation of being so the better.

Martha, with a weight on her heart, packed Philip's clothes in the sea-chest. Her mother sighed when the garments so sacred to her eyes were shut for ever from her sight. So long as Philip wore them in her house, she might put on buttons, and brush, and fold, and generally take care of them. Now they would be covered with oil-paint, she knew; for the young man was frightfully careless when excited about his picture; and though he had a kind of smock-frock to paint in, he was so wild in his ways, that frequently, when he was washed clean and, his palette and brushes having been previously purified, he was about to attack the roasted potatoes steaming below, he had squeezed out a fresh supply of his filthy colours, and gone to work again without putting on the dark blue garment at fourpence per yard, with which his future mother-in-law insisted on adorning him whenever he began his work.

The night was far advanced, and Philip was to start at two o'clock in the morning. It was very cold and dreary, though Mrs. Clemens had kept up a fire in the sitting-room, and two candles were still alight; an unheard-of extravagance in her household. Martha had packed Philip's trunk, but only he, he said, could pack his painting-materials and his easel. Luckily, the latter was fitted with hinges, and doubled-up conveniently. He was tying his brushes in bundles, with the points and ends placed alternately, to prevent the hair being bent, when Martha, having completed all she could do for his comfort in travelling, came into the painting-room to see if she could be of

any farther use. At the bottom of his japanned
painting-box there were shelves with spaces for
mill-board. One of these boards was standing up,
with its face turned to the wall. As Philip was tying up his brushes carefully, and corking-down his
bottles of drying-oil and meguilp, he saw Martha
approaching the piece of mill-board, which he had
left out to the last moment to be exposed longer
to the air, when he cried out sharply, ' *Note touche
—note droye!*' But Martha had already touched
and turned the little painting, though without
injury to its beauty, and had seen what had given
her a choking sensation in her throat and a sinking of the heart, produced by indescribable mortification. The picture was a small copy of the
portrait he had painted for Lord Tynedale, even
more ethereal in its beauty than the original; for
he had executed the head only, surrounded by
light clouds, not having had time to finish the
figure. Had Martha known more of a painter's
habits, and how frequently a slight sketch is taken
to recall the treatment of a favourite subject, she
might have been somewhat comforted; but she
saw in the copy only a romantic admiration for
the original, and it must be admitted that there
were good grounds for her uneasiness. She said

nothing, but gave up the board quietly to the
eager fingers that clutched it, whilst the painter's
eyes glanced rapidly over it, lest her touch might
have smudged any part of the copy. He had no
idea of her suffering. The feeling of worship he
felt for the original of the painting was so different from the quiet tenderness born of gratitude
which he felt for Martha, that the difference of
the feeling seemed to him to preclude the notion
of rivalry. He would have said, had the case
been put to him, that a man's betrothed ought
not to blame him if, whilst he holds her hand, he
worships a star in the firmament.

He slid the painting into its groove, dropped
the bolt, and locked the box. It was only just in
time, for he heard the wheels of the doctor's gig
and the trampling of the pale horse. The doctor
had promised to call for him, knowing that the
widow had no means of getting his portmanteau
to Seadrift Church Town, whence the coach
started. Philip took the trunk in his hands, and
went downstairs with it; Martha following with
the easel under one arm, and the painting-box in
her hand. Mrs. Clemens stood at the open door,
with a comforter in her hand which she had
knitted for Philip, and with which she straight-

way enveloped his neck. There was no light but
that of the miserable candle which flared on the
ledge in the passage. Philip, wishing to make
his adieus in proper form, said,

'Gratias, vara kindness yours, moi loave!'

He kissed Martha's cheek; then, turning to
Mrs. Clemens, he kissed her cheek also, saying,
'Moi wife!'—a mistake that sent her into a
nervous giggling, and added tears of vexation to
those of grief in the eyes of Martha; so meaning-
less to him seemed the few words of English he
had acquired, and so senseless their application.
Had he sought to kiss her last, it might have
shown some especial preference of herself above
her mother; but he was indifferent, though in-
tending to be most kind, she perceived.

'But he is engaged to be my husband,' said
Martha, clenching her hand on the finger of
which was the gold ring he had given her; 'and
I know he is the soul of truth, justice, and honour,
and he will keep his word.'

CHAPTER III.

'We that had loved him so, followed him, honour'd him,
Lived in his mild and magnificent eye.'

BROWNING.

MRS. CLEMENS shut the door, after one glance
at the lamps of the departing vehicle, that glared
at her like the eyes of a wild-beast through the
darkness.   It was all gloomy and desolate out of
doors, and as there were yet many hours to elapse
ere the twilight of morning should glimmer through
the frosted pane, both the mother and the daughter lay down on their beds; Mrs. Clemens still
simpering over Philip's mistake, Martha sick with
the uncommunicable uneasiness of jealousy.

No arrangement had been made for corre-
spondence between the engaged couple, for a
simple but unanswerable reason. Philip could·not
write anything that could be understood in English.   The few words he knew were from sound
only, and those, as had been proved, were very
illusive as to the meanings he attached to them.
Martha's letters would have been unintelligible
for the same cause.

The Beach House at Seadrift was more dreary

to Martha when she awoke about eight o'clock on
that December morning when Philip had left her,
than she had ever found it before that fatal day
when he had been cast stranded at her feet by
the reckless storm. She prepared breakfast for
her mother, whose fatigues on the previous day,
and the unusual hour to which she had been kept
awake, had made later than usual; then, before
she partook of any herself, she went into the deserted painting-room.

It was very desolate — moreover, very disor-
dered, not to say dirty; for Philip had fought
against the entrance of any dust-pan or brush
with such a torrent of remonstrances in Spanish,
he had defended his beloved paintings with ges-
ticulations so energetic, that both the women
had given way to what they imagined to be his
representations that his work would be utterly
spoilt if they swept or dusted the painting-room.
He always looked forward to the day when it
should be thoroughly purified, which was to happen at that Greek kalend when one picture should
be perfectly dry, and another not begun. Martha
looked round, and longed to see the former inmate
in the chair that had been pushed impatiently out
out of the way when he had packed his mate-

rials. Sketches were lying about which he had
not cared to take with him—bits of the cloisters
of the Spanish convent; and a peasant woman, in
red jacket and purple petticoat, leant languidly
against the gray stone entrance till one of the
fathers should hear her application. Another was
a procession of monks pacing up the chapel towards the high altar, and the acolytes swinging
their censers. Philip, tongue-tied by his ignorance of English, communicated his memories of
the past to paper. He had liked his sketches at
the moment he had executed them; for, as De
Fresnoy says, the artist who makes a design is
like an ape who hath just brought forth her
young, in which, however frightful may be her
progeny, she seeth no fault, but believeth it to be
perfection. Therefore, that sage writer advises
every artist to put aside his design for a few
weeks, or even months, when its infirmities will
stand out naked to his eye, without the interven-
tion of the veil interposed by self-conceit.

The sketches were good, however, and would
have stood the test of time ; but the one oil copy
of the girl occupied all his thoughts, and the
sketches were thrown away to give her more space.
Martha's care of them arose from her devotion to

the artist. She suspected that they were but poor performances. They were so very unlike the painting she had executed on velvet at school, that she regarded them with a kind of tender pity that Philip could do no better. The little blotches of colour which stood for the figure and face of the woman at the entrance of the cloisters, she believed a good painter would have finished highly, though the object was supposed to stand at a distance, which in reality would have made all details invisible. Poor Philip was doomed to have his diamonds taken for glass—a common fate.

CHAPTER IV.

'I see some sparkles of a better hope.'

WHEN Martha came down to breakfast, after having confiscated the discarded sketches, she found her mother in a cheerful state, and full of anticipations of wealth and good luck in the future.

She had still some money left in her pocket, which gave her a feeling of comfort and importance. The young man, long looked for, had come at last; and though he had seemed at first to be

a dependent on their bounty, he was now about to
be rich, and her son-in-law, all in due time. That
he would change his mind, and break his engagement, she, in the faith and honesty of her disposition, did not anticipate. *Her* old man, when once
he had told his love, never cared for any other
girl. Mrs. Clemens had felt grievous hardships
in her life; but want of truth to her had not been
one; so she anticipated no recalcitration from
Philip. Besides, who would not be delighted to
fulfil an engagement with such a comely clever
girl as Martha—and so good too!

'To be sure, Martha my dear,' said Mrs. Clemens, addressing her daughter, 'one can't have
everything in this world; and I should have preferred a young gentleman that wasn't a Papist;
for 'tis sad to see, them as hasn't got chapels that
please them nigh at hand, seem to me to forget
to worship altogether. I did hope, as there was
no Catholic chapel handier than Plymouth, that if
he had waited a little longer, we might have got
Mr. Rose to go with us to the meeting-house.'

'Where would have been the use of that, mother, when he could not have understood a word
that Mr. Damnall said?—and no pleasure, if he
had.'

'Ah, poor boy! he was slow at his English; and I fear he won't learn much good in those foreign places. I take it they don't talk like Christians there; and, to tell the truth, Martha, when Philip himself talked fast, it always put me in mind of the jabbering of an ape your dear father brought once from the Ingies.'

'Most likely Mr. Rose thought the same of your talking, mother.'

'O, no; he could not do that, because we talk right — like everybody else. But, child, look there!—there's two ladies coming along over the beach. I really believe they are coming to our house.'

'I wish they would stay away,' said Martha peevishly, 'whoever they are, when there is so much to be done in cleaning the house. 'Tis Mrs. Deal and her daughter, I see,' she continued. 'They are not likely to want to see *me*, so I will leave you to find out why they have come.'

Martha, with keen resentment still brooding in her mind as to the small insults they had contrived to inflict on her during their former interview, had no wish to subject herself to a repetition of them. Yet she could scarcely help listening to the conversation downstairs.

'I hope we don't inconvenience you, mem, a-calling so early,' said the contralto tones of Mrs. Deal, glancing round at the uncleared-away tokens of breakfast.

'We are rather late,' replied Mrs. Clemens, rather crestfallen. 'I assure you, 'tis quite unusual, ma'am; but we was up till three o'clock this morning to give my son-in-law that is to be his breakfast.'

'Indeed, mum!' rejoined Mrs. Deal, who knew the fact as well as Mrs. Clemens, having called at the coach-office on the previous day, and seen the way-bill.

'And where is Martha, Mrs. Clemens?' sang the clear birdlike tones of the fair Julia.

'Poor girl! I'm sure I feel for her!' with a heavy sigh. 'Eyes and nose red, no doubt; don't like to show,' said Mrs. Deal. 'Young folks do feel like that; not that Martha can be said to be what one may call a girl—so I daresay she don't take on so much.'

'Martha is very well, thank you, ma'am; and her eyes and nose is much as usual.'

'I'm glad to hear it, Mrs. Clemens. Her eyes is what I partikalar want, and her nose is no matter, specially as her young man is gone—nobody else is likely to look at her; so p'r'aps you'll call her down.'

Mrs. Clemens was not used to contend; so she went up, and found Martha putting on a clean collar preparatory to seeing her visitors, as she knew how the contest would terminate, from her mother's usual timidity and natural habit of yielding.

'O, Martha, I am so glad to see you again,' said the young lady. 'I knew you would be in affliction, my dear, and glad to have the solace of friendship. And so *he* is gone!

> ' And is he gone? On sudden solitude
> How oft that fearful question would intrude!
> 'Twas but a moment past and there he stood.'

Do you not often quote those affecting lines, my dear Martha?'

'Would you believe it,' said Mrs. Deal, addressing Mrs. Clemens, having begun the subject most interesting to herself, 'the last flannel petitcoat as I had made was—' and she made an emphatic pause.

'Are you not wretched lest he should be—'

'Gored,' interposed the mother emphatically.

'Faithless?' said the daughter plaintively. 'You know there is "the high dàma's brow more melancholy, and the peasant's cheek of ruddy bronze;" and we, my dear Martha, are but pale unripened beauties of the north.'

Julia said this with a triumphant disclaimer in her expression; for her face resembled Byron's description of the Italian peasant's beauty—bright, vivid, and piquant; and of this she was perfectly aware.

'Would you believe it, Mrs. Clemens,' said the matron, 'the dressmakers at Plymouth have made Julia's dress full all round—all but a bit as long as my finger in the front?'

'Indeed, mem! It must make folks look broad about the hips, I should think.'

'Has he left you no picture of himself, my sweet friend? You know—'

'Dutch-built, as my husband used to say.'

> '—The limner's art may paint the absent feature,
>   And give the eye of distant weeping faith
>   To view the form of its idolatry.'

'No,' said Martha bluntly, 'he left me no likeness of himself. He is not likely to forget me; and he knows I shall not forget him, picture or no picture.'

'Ah, that can't be trusted; it won't wash,' said Mrs. Deal, pointing to one of many patterns she had brought, ostensibly to choose a gown for herself; really to prove what a wonderful assortment of new articles her husband had procured from Plymouth.

'Dear, ma!' said Julia, with a giggle, 'it do come in so queer what you are saying! But I daresay Martha ain't to be took down about her sweetheart; and I must say he's worth the keeping—so 'ansome, so dark and melancholy; I am sure there are some mysteries about him. Did that ever strike you, Martha dear?'

'I know nothing about mistresses, I'm sure,' said Mrs. Clemens, thinking it her duty to come to the front in defence of Martha, who appeared to be unusually silent; 'but he is as quiet and well-disposed a young man as I ever saw, and I am quite content to have him for a son-in-law. 'Tis not every young man so clever that a great lord will spend three hundred pounds in a year on his edication.'

'Three hundred pounds a year!' cried the women. But recovering after a pause, 'Yes, mum; what you said is right as to the money; but what do you think of his immortal soul? It can't be pleasant to you to know that he is a castaway, and must go to the worm that dieth not and the fire that is not quenched in the next world,' said Mrs. Deal.

'I don't know what you mean, ma'am,' replied Mrs. Clemens, looking both offended and disturbed at the prospect looming in the distance of Philip's fate. 'He's never done no wrong that I know of; and as to his mistresses, I never heard of them before.'

'Mysteries, not mistresses, I said,' cried the clear shrill voice of Miss Julia. 'Dear, dear Mrs. Clemens!'

'Well, mysteries or mistresses, 'tis all one—or ought to be; and I don't believe Mr. Rose will go to hot places any more than—than yourself, Miss Deal.'

'I would not hurt your feelings, mum,' said Mrs. Deal, 'but I can't have my daughter evened with a young man that Mr. Damnall said in his discourse last Sunday evening was given over to work all uncleanness with greediness.'

'What do he mean by that? He've not been upstairs to the painting-room, have he?' said the conscience-stricken advocate of the absent, feeling that in some unsuspected manner the secrets of that uncleansed retreat had become known to her minister.

Mrs. Deal looked at her with bewildered horror in her looks. What atrocities might not have been perpetrated in that room, from the notice of which Mrs. Clemens seemed to shrink! Miss Julia, though on the watch for a mystery, was sharper than her mother, and saw the mistake.

'Mr. Damnall did not mean the pollutions of the outer man, Mrs. Clemens, by filthy oil-paints and turpentine, and suchlike; but the worship of the Scarlet Woman, who sits on seven hills.'

'She do,' asserted Mrs. Deal; 'and a wonderful figger she must be to cover so much; though 'tain't likely to be a comfortable seat, in my opinion. You *must* know, both of you, that the young man never went to a place of worship all the three months he lived at Seadrift; and now he's gone to the very head-quarters of all abominations—to Rome itself.'

'Ah,' said Julia, 'he's in the fashion; for Mr. Damnall said a great many lost souls had gone over to Rome lately.'

'Excuse me, Miss Julia, but did you call this morning to inquire after Mr. Rose's soul, or is there anything else you wish to know?' said Martha, who, having no play of fancy, was rather like a sledge-hammer in her methods of proceeding.

She saw something carefully wrapped in a piece of white calico, which looked like a dress.

'Yes,' said Mrs. Deal; 'we've brought Julia's silk dress, that is just come from Plymouth; and a sweet merino, for you to make up on the pattern, my dear. You see, 'tis a new fashion; and I daresay you will be glad to make it up at half-price, for the advantage it must be to a dressmaker to have a dress really well cut at last. I should like you to take the pattern at once, that it may not get dirty in your house.'

Mrs. Clemens looked round, and sniffed with her nose in the air.

'I cannot make it up at all, Miss Julia. My time is too much occupied.'

'*Indeed!*' said the bright Julia indignantly. 'How so?'

'We go to Norfolk almost immediately.'

'Yes; and I am sure the house wants a good doing before the London gentleman comes—*if* he is coming,' suggested Mrs. Deal.

'It is to be thoroughly painted and whitewashed,' said the widow.

'Does he bring his furniture, mem? I suppose so; for 'tis not likely he would be contented with yours, if he is well to do in the world.'

'That is his own affair, and nobody else's,' said the widow.

'He is a bachelor, I think?' said Julia.

'Yes, miss; and if you can catch him for a husband, the better for you, though he is old. 'Tis not every girl can get a handsome young man like my Martha here,' added the mother, with a look of triumph.

'Umph! though he is a Papist, mum,' suggested the wife. 'But I don't wonder that *your* daughter caught at the young man.'

'Lor, mother, don't talk!' said Miss Julia, in an unusual fit of candour. 'Mr. Rose is a beautiful young man, and, Papist or not, I should have been glad of him for my beau. I could say, like the devoted Hinda:

> " Thou for my sake at Alla's shrine ;
> And I at any god's for thine." '

Mrs. Deal lingered.

'Mrs. Clemens, do you find linen, sheets, tablecloths, piller-cases, towels, dinner-napkins? You know you can't have half that a gentleman must want. Any way, you might name Mr. Deal to the gentleman that's coming; and I'll warrant Julia and I will make 'em up in no time.'

'I'm of opinion, mum,' replied the widow loftily,

'that a gentleman coming from Newcastle can't want coals; and that a merchant living in London city could get what he wants there instead of coming down to buy of Mr. Deal.'

'Well, mum, you needn't take me up so! I only thought it might be convenient to know that Mr. Deal has a fresh assortment of goods down, of best quality and reasonable prices; but I am a good-natured fool to demean myself by talking to you, when I might have spoken to Mrs. Mereside, who is quite the lady, if she do speak up sharp now and then.'

'By-by, Martha,' said Julia; 'I wish you good luck "to lure your tassel gentle back again." 'Tain't easy when birds are flown.'

'That is true, Miss Julia,' observed the widow; 'tassels are genteel, and Martha sewed them on the ends of your scarf quite firm to match the sleeves, so I can't see how they should fly off. Very likely the sewing silk was rotten; she bought it at Mr. Deal's shop.'

'Your ma is as deaf as a post, my dear Martha; she don't understand anything; but it don't matter. Good-bye, sweet Martha.'

Martha gave a cold response, and Mrs. Deal carried the new dress back, carefully shrouded in its calico-covering, growing more angry with Martha for not taking a pattern, as she felt herself to have been uselessly inconvenienced by its bulk.

Martha and her mother had enough to do in cleaning the house before the workmen came in to paint, paper, and to whitewash it. Very useless was this feminine industry when their dirty shoes were to pollute the scrubbed floors; but it was a point of conscience with Mrs. Clemens, and with Martha also.

CHAPTER V.

' Is Folly, then, so old ? Why, let us see
About what time of life may Folly be.'
W. SPENSER.

MARTHA shrank from the thought of leaving the Beach House; she clung to the recollections of her home, and to the scenes where she had lived with Philip. She had never seen her aunt, and could not have any of the tender remembrances, in which her mother seemed to revel, of early youth passed with sister Betsy. Mrs. Clemens, forgetful of the lapse of time, thought of sister Betsy as she had last seen her, the beautiful bride of a wealthy man. She was never tired of describing the brilliancy of her skin and the splendour of her eyes.

'But she is old now, mother,' Martha would suggest.

'Old, indeed! I don't know what *you* call old,' said the widow, bridling; 'she is three years younger than I am.'

'But that is too old for—' beauty, Martha was about to add, but substituted the word 'bloom.' Then observing her mother's look of displeasure, she said, 'Delicate round features last much longer, mother; and I daresay you are handsomer now than your sister is.'

It was not often that Martha condescended to flatter, and the pretty speech was appreciated the more for its rarity. Mrs. Clemens' face expanded into a smile, and she sat herself up and threw her head back as she had done when she expected that Philip was about to paint her.

'You have your best dress on, mother,' observed Martha, seeing for the first time that her mother had on her Sunday clothes. 'I suppose the ordinary ones were wet with scrubbing.'

'Well, they *were* wet,' said the widow, looking rather conscious and frightened; 'but the truth is, that I half promised to take a dish of tea with Mrs. Bolitho, and if you would not mind being left, Martha, this dark evening, I should like to go.'

'I do not mind, at all,' replied the daughter, thinking how intense would be the comfort of a few hours to herself spent in uninterrupted leisure, for the cleansing processes had been conscientiously gone through. 'But, mother, about your returning: I cannot have you coming at night over the broken causeway.'

'No, my dear, no. Mrs. Bolitho has got to send for a passenger by the mail, and the chaise will bring me round, and then go back to take him up.'

Martha smiled to think how completely the matter had been arranged without consulting her, and guessed at the truth—which was that Mrs. Bolitho wanted to hear all that could be gleaned of their future plans, and of the new tenant at Beach House; and her mother was equally anxious to hear something of Lord Tynedale's sayings and doings. In truth, Martha was not without some curiosity herself to find out anything relating to his lordship's young relative, the original of that disquieting picture; and it was possible that observations might be made on Philip which would interest his betrothed.

So at half-past three o'clock in the afternoon she attended her mother, seeing her safely over the pebbly shore and into Mrs. Bolitho's garden; then, her duties performed for the evening, she returned across the beach and took her way far round the bay away from human dwellings, where the gulls and the sea-mews were her only companions. The long melancholy cries of the seabirds impressed her with sadness. She had wandered to a part of the shore where sand took the place of pebbles, and was conscious she had gone as far as she dared in the fast-decreasing light; but she need not return home yet. There was an idea of black horror in the empty house now, in all its silence and neatness, as if it were the abode of death. There seemed something portentously gloomy in the night; and she sat as if fascinated on a fragment of rock, listening to the recurring roar of the waves as they dashed themselves on the shore, and ran up, depositing their surge of yellow foam at her feet. She feared them not; she knew that the tide was receding.

As the gloom increased in intensity, nothing remained visible but the mighty mass of granite called the Gull Rock, up to the base of which the billows rushed, and sprang into the air, broken into a myriad jets of white spray.

This was the rock so fatal to vessels. Not

only did its dark sides oppose themselves jaggedly to those fragile fabrics at high water, but its foundations sloped to some distance out into the ocean; so that seamen unaccustomed to the coast found themselves suddenly in shoal water where they had counted on deep sea.

It was on the Gull Rock that the Spanish vessel had foundered when Philip had been washed on shore; it was against the Gull Rock that her father's bark had been driven and shattered to fragments, leaving her without a parent or brothers. Her mother's plaintive melody seemed to ring in her ears with the words,

> 'Why do they say, "In Nature
> Is nothing made in vain"?
> And why beneath the water
> These hideous rocks remain?'

As she gazed on this mighty giant, standing unmoved for centuries amidst the ocean, and as careless of the human lives it demolished as of the half-fledged sea-birds tossed by wild winds out of their fragile nests, which the parents had hidden in the clefts of the rock, Martha's spirits were weighed down by the conviction, that, in some way to her inscrutable, the Gull Rock, the only object visible through the darkening air from its contrast with the shrouding foam, was to be mixed up with her fate.

She regarded it steadfastly till her eyes grew dim and her heavy head sank between her hands. She distinguished no sound excepting the continuous roar of the ever - advancing body of waves dashing themselves on the shore, and their hissing retreat as they were sucked back into the main with their load of sand and shingle, till a sad voice close to her, which seemed like the wail of a spirit, said,

' She will die.'

She took her hands from her face, and arose. Standing near her was a tall youth between sixteen and seventeen years of age, who had been considered by the elders of her sect as inspired by Heaven to preach the Gospel and to prophesy.

'The young men shall see visions, the old men shall dream dreams,' they had said; and the latter days, when these things should happen, had come. After a short time he had shown decided symptoms of insanity, and had not been permitted to address the congregation on the Sabbath; but he was still considered ' an innocent' inspired by Heaven, and his prophecies and denunciations were listened to with some amount of reverence and awe. As he was known to be harmless, he wandered about without restraint or superintendence.

He was seemingly unconscious of Martha's proximity, and was gazing, as she had done, on the tumbled billows as they broke on the Gull Rock, standing with his dark hair dishevelled by the night wind, half shrouded in darkness and mist, and his wild eyes flashing with the light of madness.

Martha was not free from the superstition of persons of her class. It seemed to her that the prescience of her fate which had depressed her might now be dissipated or confirmed.

She stood up, saying,

'Micah Dias, who will die?'

The voice replied, with looks searching intently the dim horizon,

'Martha Clemens! Alas, woe is me!'

'When—where?' she cried.

The youth shook his hand impatiently towards the horizon, and passed away into the darkness.

Martha stood silently for a short time. Her mind had been wrought up into a feeling of desperation, almost of defiance of fate, when she had asked the question. Now a cold shuddering seized her, as if she already felt the swirl of the rushing water over her head. She was chilled even to the marrow of her bones. The hour, the spot, her previous presentiments, all concurred in oppressing her with dread. She had nerved herself to ask the secret of futurity, and the answer had been adverse.

They were to sail on the following morning. Was her life to end so soon? She knew not, nor dared she confront the image of death alone. She would go home, and trust that her mother would soon return to bring news from life and living creatures, and make her forget the vague terrors of the night.

CHAPTER VI.

'All within is young and glowing,
Spite of old age's outward showing.'

HORACE SMITH.

WHEN she reached Beach House, Martha sat down outside the door to listen for the wheels of the post-chaise which was to bring Mrs. Clemens. She hoped to hear these coming more distinctly from the road, as the tide was now far down on the beach, and the roar of the waves less audible. She dared not enter. The empty house was too full of shadows to be encountered alone, and too destitute of subjects of occupation by which they might be chased.

At length, O joy! the rumbling of the crazy vehicle was heard turning the corner of the road, and Martha could distinguish the steps being let down. Then she went along the garden-path, and met her mother, happy in the social evening she had passed, and rustling in all the importance of her best gown.

'O, mother,' cried Martha in a sudden burst of tenderness, 'I hope you will live as long as I do! What would the world be without you?'

'Think of Mr. Rose, my dear; and perhaps a little Martha or a little Philip to be a comfort to your age, as you are to mine. Dear, dear! I hope Mr. John the coachman kept my gown off the wheels! So dirty as the roads are!'

'So you have had a pleasant evening, mother?' said Martha, anxious to forget that which she had passed, and, in that desire, becoming uncharacteristically talkative.

'Yes, my dear, yes; Mrs. Bolitho was very kind. We was all alone only just at the end, before I came away. She took out her best chany teacups and silver teapot, as was a wonder to look

at, 'twas so bright; and rounds of toast with fresh
butter. 'Tis to be hoped Captain Bolitho drives
a roaring trade. But some folks have all the
luck; and I was well-to-do when your poor father was alive; but best off in having *him*,' added
the widow, and her voice trembled a little. ' 'Tis
of no use thinking of that. And, Martha, if you
could but see how your likeness looks now! 'Tis
in the beautifulest frame!—so wide all round, and
so bright, and worked with gold patterns! When
my lord went into his bedroom to dress, Mrs. Bolitho took me up into the drawing-room where
he sits, and on one chair there was the picture of
you, and on another the Shipwreck, in a handsome frame also. But, lor! looking at the picture
of them waves and the black night and the black
sky, and the terrible red light up at the top of
the cliff, which ain't there really, and thinking of
our voyage to Lynn to-morrow morning, made
me so uncomfortable, that says I, "I don't say nothing against my son-in-law that is to be; but why
he should paint such dreadful things I can't tell,
unless 'tis to make folks feel cold water run down
their backs—and that might do in summer, but
not now." So, my dear, I gave another look at
the picture of you, and says I, " 'Tis like an angel,

Mrs. Bolitho, 'tis so bright and beautiful." " Go along with you!" said she. " Them painters—" But she didn't go on; for my eyes had gone over to the table, where my lord's snuff-box lay all worked with gold and diamonds on the top, and a cambric handkerchief, as was worth a guinea if 'twas worth a penny, and smelling of sweet flowers beautiful. " Yes, mum," says she, " and Mr. James tells me that my lord orders three dozen at a time. Look at that little crown in the corner; that's 'cause he's a lord. And the young lady, though she's so young, she won't be behind my lord; and hers are thirty shillings each; and her maid gets rare pickings; for Miss is but a child, and loses her things as fast as she gets them; but my lord will never say her nay." '

' Where is she now ?' said Martha.

' O, in one of my lord's great houses. She has a French governess and an English one, and they fight like two cats. They do say, Mr. James told Mrs. Bolitho, that my lord and a young lord's father—a great earl—mean to make up a match between his eldest son and this young lady, when she is old enough.'

' O !' said Martha in a tone of relief. ' Does she like him ?'

'Well enough, they say; only he is a quiet well-behaved young man, and she is always so lively—dancing, singing, or learning poetry all day. She will drive him crazy, they say, or he will give her the mopes. But he is very rich, and so is she, and, as Mrs. Bolitho said, money makes money. Then Mrs. Bolitho was very kind, and seemed so anxious that we should be comfortable in Norfolk, and that my sister should be kind to us, and how much money she had, and all that. But you know, Martha my dear, I could not tell her, for I don't know myself. Then Mr. James came in when he had seen my lord into bed, and we had a bowl of punch, for Mrs. Bolitho likes to have things comfortable about her; and then the chaise came to the door, and, would you believe it, Mr. James handed me in as if I was the greatest lady in the land, and stood with his hat off till the chaise drove off.'

' 'Tis time, mother, to go to bed; we must rise in the dark to-morrow morning. This is our last evening in our own house.'

'True, my dear,' responded the more cheerful mother; 'but you see I shall make a good penny by letting it, and if we live, we may come back— some day when poor Betsy is no more—and be more comfortable. I wonder if Betsy has a silver teapot and chany?' she said meditatively; with an eye to future inheritance, and to a glorious vista of tea-drinkings with Mrs. Bolitho as a guest.

CHAPTER VII.

'For Satan, wiser than before,
Now tempts by making rich, not making poor.'

MARTHA slept little, and was up in sufficient time to make a cup of tea for her mother before they left the house. Then the contents of the tea-tray were carefully cleaned and put into the cupboard, and they dragged their boxes outside the door to be ready for the boatman, who was to fetch them. The key of the house was concealed under a large stone, whence it was to be taken by Mrs. Mereside, by previous agreement. The gruff voices of the men were now heard, and the women followed them to the water's edge. The gleam of a torch lighted the dancing waves, and distracted the unaccustomed eyes of the mother and daughter. Martha was too anxious lest Mrs. Clemens should lose her footing to have room for apprehension for herself till they were both seated together in the heavily-laden boat, when the water rising to its edge, and terrible in its blackness, made Martha think of the prophecy uttered by Micah Dias; but no catastrophe befell them. They reached the vessel in safety, and three days after arrived, without more damage than that which resulted from sea-sickness and fatigue, at the port of King's Lynn; and shortly after a hack conveyance deposited them at the house of Mrs. Clemens' sister, Mrs. Betsy Carden.

'Betsy does live in a grand house, don't she?' whispered Mrs. Clemens to her daughter, as they ascended the flight of stone steps which led to the large oak door studded with nails.

Martha assented, thinking that, though magnificent in size, the house looked gloomy. If that was the impression outside, it was greatly increased when an old maid-servant opened the door, with such apparent unwillingness that it would have seemed as if she dreaded the incursion of an enemy.

'Where is my sister—Mrs. Carden?' cried the widow impatiently.

They stood in a fine oak hall, of which the colour was nearly black, hung round at the cornice with wreaths of carved flowers and fruits of the same material. The floor was oak, the ceiling and walls were of oak; and of oak was the grand old staircase, ornamented with Cupids and monsters, ' hydras and chimeras dire,' carved also of oak.

When Mrs. Clemens had exclaimed, 'Where is my sister?' the old vinegar-faced servant turned her head by way of answer and looked towards the staircase, whence descended a tall slim woman, beautiful even in age and sickness, who moved deliberately, not to slip on the polished oak.

Betsy Carden was about to greet a long lost and beloved sister after the lapse of twenty-seven years; but she did not move swiftly to welcome her. When the sisters stood face to face, they regarded each other with a troubled expression. Mrs. Clemens could not believe that the slender woman before her was the blooming girl she had last beheld as a bride. Mrs. Carden could not be certain that the small, pink (but shrivelled) cheeked old woman who stood on her threshold was the comely matron who had borne to the font the infant Martha, to whom Mrs. Carden herself had been sponsor.

————

CHAPTER VIII.

'We see Time's furrows on another brow ;
  How few themselves in that just mirror see !'
                                    YOUNG.

'BETSY !' said Mrs. Clemens, 'is it you?'

'O, *'tis* Nancy Clemens, then,' said Mrs. Carden; and she slightly offered her cheek to be kissed
by her sister. 'And this is my goddaughter Martha, I suppose; you have grown a deal since I
held you in my arms, young woman.' No kiss
was offered to Martha, and none desired. If Mrs.
Carden thought she would have a malleable character to fashion in this woman, who had almost
a masculine strength of mind from the necessity of
being the person to act in all emergencies, she
would find herself mistaken.

The first feeling in the breast of Martha was
that her aunt was not ill, and that for some inscrutable reason she had brought herself and her
mother there under false pretences. The second
was resentment for the coldness of her greeting to
her guests, come so great a distance for her accom-
modation. Martha was by no means a gracious
person herself, but she could not brook the absence
of civility in others. Being of a slow and sullen

temperament, however, she followed her mother in silence on her aunt saying to Mrs. Clemens,

'You had better come up and take off your bonnet, Nancy.'

'What is to be done with all this rub—luggish —luggage, I mean,' said the cross old servant; 'and here is the man wants to be paid.'

'*I* will pay the man,' said Martha; 'seemingly I had better add a sixpence to what is owed, that he may take the boxes to our room.'

Mrs. Carden stopped, and finally returned to the door, leaving her sister on the stairs.

'Ruth,' said she, 'see that the man takes off his shoes, and observe that he takes particular care that the sides and corners of the trunks do not touch the walls as he goes up.'

The boxes were carried up the back stairs, Ruth following them with Argus eyes; and entering by another door, Mrs. Carden conducted her guests to their bedrooms, and met the peccant trunks and the porter in the middle of the room.

'You *have* touched the wall,' said Mrs. Carden sternly to the man. 'What do you mean by such carelessness?' and she pointed to some yellow powder on the corner of one of the boxes. The

man scratched his head in silence, as Martha gave
him enough to satisfy him.

'Ruth will bring you hot water,' said Mrs.
Carden; 'when you have washed, she will conduct you to the room where I sit.'

Thus saying, she left the mother and daughter
alone, shutting the door; on which Mrs. Clemens
sat down and began to cry.

'O, Martha, who would ever have thought of
Betsy being like that?'

'How did you expect to find her, mother?
Young and beautiful, as you saw her twenty-seven
years ago?' replied the daughter, who was always
irritated by her mother's tears, and chose to ignore
the coldness of their reception.

'You know what I mean, my dear,' said Mrs.
Clemens, wiping her eyes; 'so cold and uncivil
like.'

'Look, mother, what a handsome bed!' said
Martha, knowing how to turn the current of her
thoughts; 'real damask curtains! Very old, dropping to pieces. I'd darn that rent, if I had some
crimson sewing silk.'

'Dear, dear! so it is handsome; and look at the
bedposts, Martha; such carving! And all this belongs to Betsy!' exclaimed the simple woman, taking

some comfort in the idea that a relative of hers should have such possessions.

Ruth entered in the midst of this inspection, and made both the mother and daughter look foolish at being detected.

'Here is the hot water,' she said curtly, setting down a large canful; and returning to her mistress she told what she had seen, and observed,

'They are counting over the treasures they shall have when you are gone, mum.'

'They can wait,' said Mrs. Carden, by no means disturbed by the aspect with which Ruth regarded matters. 'One thing is certain: I can't take a carved mahogany bed and silk-damask curtains into the next world with me; and 'tis more natural that my own kith and kin should inherit than a stranger in blood,' she added, looking at Ruth fixedly.

Ruth did not like that look, and she retired, muttering,

'I am sure *I* don't want your goods.'

In the mean time Martha had gone on her knees and uncorded the boxes; and then she took from one of slighter fabric her mother's best cap, with the bow of gray ribbons and the well-plaited border; and both women, having enjoyed the warmth and abundance of the water, after the deprivation of shipboard, dressed themselves in clean garments, and descended the stairs to try to find their hostess. They went hand-in-hand, and started when the large clock told the hour in a deep sonorous tone—four o'clock.

The month was February, and they shivered with awe and with cold as they trod those strange stairs in the dim twilight. Martha felt a longing to see some means of egress, and lifted a green-gauze curtain which tended to increase the gloom of a window, which the atmosphere had already incrusted with frost. She felt like a strange cat watching for some means of escape, though by doing so her discomfort might be increased. The window presented the view of an old garden, venerable with gray stone vases and urns, which Nature had done her best to ornament with her rainbow-tinted mosses, scarlet, orange, and green. Over them large cedars spread their protecting arms, making by their undisturbed heaps of with-ered fibres a soft footing for those who chose to wander in their sombre avenues.

Her glimpse was a hurried one; for Ruth, like a shepherd's dog who has charge of two stray sheep, came to drive them into the presence of Mrs. Carden.

They found her sitting upright on one side of the fire, busily employed in knitting ·squares for a counterpane. The chair was not turned towards the chimney, but stood with its back to the wall. There was one of precisely the same size and pattern, with the same high carved back, on the opposite side of the chimney, and Mrs. Carden, pointing to it, said:

'Sit there, Nancy.'

Nancy was not aware how great was the honour conferred on her; for that had been the seat in which the deceased Mr. Carden had been permitted to rest his weary limbs for some years, when his business for the day had been concluded.

Martha looked round for a resting-place for herself, and was about to draw from its position against the wall one of these massive pieces of furniture, when the voice of her aunt arrested her:

·'You must not remove that chair; it destroys the harmony of the room, and makes it untidy. You may sit on it where it is, if you please, or on this ottoman.'

Martha, shivering with the cold of a twilight in February, preferred the ottoman.

'It is five minutes past four o'clock,' said Mrs. Betsy Carden deliberately. 'Dinner will be ready at six o'clock. You will not require refreshment till then?'

Poor Mrs. Clemens, who had suffered so much from sea-sickness and giddiness as to have been unable to eat anything on board the vessel, and was just beginning to feel the return of appetite, heard this announcement with dismay and in silence. Martha, who judged her mother's cravings by her own, and could not endure that Mrs. Clemens should suffer, if she did, said:

'Aunt, my mother is exhausted, and requires food, which she has been unable to take for the last three days. You must give her some, if you do not wish to have an invalid on your hands; a discomfort both to you and to herself.'

Mrs. Carden groaned, and rising slowly, unlocked a cupboard, and took from it a bottle and a wine-glass and a box of biscuits. She placed three on a sheet of writing-paper and gave to her sister with a glassful of some cordial, and offered the same to Martha, who took the biscuits and declined the spirits.

'I am young, and do not require stimulants,' said she.

'True, you do not,' said her aunt; 'but I fancied that it was one word for your mother, and two for yourself.'

To this innuendo Martha replied not; and Mrs. Clemens, inwardly comforted by the spirits and biscuits, expanded into a benevolent smile, and was inclined to see life under that rose-coloured aspect, which Captain Morris describes as the pleasant result of potations.

'To be sure, Betsy, 'tis a comfort after being so sick—O, so sick!' said the poor woman, melted at the recollection of her own sufferings—'to come and find you in such a beautiful house, and everything so handsome about you.'

Mrs. Carden looked around gloomily.

'Yes, handsome enough; but I have seen them so long, that I cease to observe their beauty.'

'Well, but you would not like to lose them.'

'No, probably not.'

And she let her hands drop on her lap, and gave herself up to a dreamy reverie.

Mrs. Clemens had been too long away from her sister to feel any of those cobweb sources of mutual interest extending themselves between near neighbours in constant communion, which, though so fragile that the first breeze sweeps them away, are daily renewing. So they inquired of each other the fate of different schoolfellows, without caring particularly to hear of the fortunes of any, and then relapsed into silence.

In silence the mother and daughter heard the awful chime of the clock from the gloomy unlighted hall striking five, and thought with unexpressed dismay that there was another hour before they could have any chance of a comfortable meal.

It had become quite dark now, excepting the light from the embers,—too dark even for knitting; so Mrs. Carden leant back against that uncompromising chair, which gave support to the shoulders without the spectator being aware of the circumstance, so upright was the sitter, like a faithful friend, who props up his companion by effectual aid, without seeming to the world to do so. Mrs. Clemens sat in the opposite one, and Martha retreated from her ottoman to another. Her face was scorched, and every woman—whether brunette or blonde—has a tenderness for her complexion.

There she sat, and meditated on Seadrift;
on the billows beating up under the windows
of Beach House; of the fate predicted to her by
Micah Dias; of her affianced husband so far removed from her. Sometimes the flame of the
decaying fire leapt up, and showed the emblazoned
patterns on the dark leather with which the room
was hung,—birds, flowers, and wild creatures, that
had existed only in the traditions of the Chinese
Empire, and could have been represented only by
one of its sons.

The silence was broken only by some chance
question from her mother, answered briefly by her
aunt. At length the clock chimed the half hour;
then, after an interval which seemed interminable,
the three-quarters.

'Are you ready for dinner?' asked Mrs.
Carden.

'I wonder whether she expects us to wash all
over again?' thought Martha.

Mrs. Clemens meekly said she was quite
ready.

'I am not,' said the hostess; and left the
room.

'Good lawk, Martha! did you ever, my poor
child!' said Mrs. Clemens, thinking more of Mar-

tha's dulness than her own, and full of pity for
having inflicted such a situation on her.

'Mother,' said Martha, 'we have been here
just one hour and three-quarters, and 'tis longer
than all the twenty-seven years of my life before.
Can we ever get accustomed to it? I don't believe she is ill a bit. O dear! we have spent all
the money I earned in coming to this dreadful
place !'

'Hush !' said Mrs. Clemens; 'that woman Ruth
is coming to fetch us. I wonder what we shall
have for dinner?'

There was comfort in the thought; and they
followed their ancient handmaiden to the dining-
room, where the mistress of the house was already
seated.

. On the covers being removed by Ruth, seven
large mutton-chops were revealed in one dish, and
three potatoes in another. Mrs. Carden scrutin-
ised the size of each portion of the viands, and
gave the guests the two larger chops and potatoes,
keeping the smaller ones for herself. As the widow
and her daughter were hungry, they did full
justice to their food, devouring every particle
which clung to the bone, and eating even the fat
end. They seldom had afforded themselves ani-

mal food at home, and its consumption was agreeable rather than not; but they had been accustomed to a liberal, not to say unlimited, supply of potatoes, and did not approve either the quantity or the quality of those supplied to them.

'Dear! Betsy, your potatoes ain't worthy to be named in the same day with ours,' said Mrs. Clemens.

'They are the best that Lynn market can produce,' said her sister, rather offended.

Then there was a silence; which lasted till a pudding of innocent concoction was placed on the table. This Mrs. Carden seriously meditated over, and ultimately divided into three portions, and distributed to her guests and herself. The meditation, which took place with an uplifted spoon in her hand, seemed intended for the purpose of deciding how to divide it both neatly and equitably, but really resulted from the hostess thinking of other things. Neither wine nor beer appeared.

The meal, however, was not destitute of attractions. The damask tablecloth and napkins were of ·the finest quality, and spotless. The richly-chased silver was well kept, and cleaned to its utmost brightness; and there was an atmosphere of tranquillity and order, which, though it seemed

dull to the poverty-nurtured couple, was not without its charms to them. The dining-room was ill
lighted by two wax-candles only; and seeing that
the walls were in this room also covered with dark
embossed leather, the quantity of illumination they
reflected was but small.

When the meal was concluded, Mrs. Carden
led her sister and niece back to the sitting-room,
when she inquired of the pair whether they had
brought any needlework with which they might
amuse themselves.

Martha answered that her mother's eyes were
useless as regarded such an occupation, and that
rest from a task by which she had earned their
daily bread was the amusement she most coveted.

'Indeed! Then you shall read aloud one of
Smallridge's sermons,' said her aunt, who arranged
one of the two candles near to Martha, and took
the other to throw light on her knitting.

Martha read badly; she was not either quick
at catching the meaning of a sentence, or deep
enough to understand it when caught. She droned
on, and saw that her mother's chin reclined on her
breast, as she sat in the high-backed chair. A
small table—such as was formerly used to hold
a wineglass and decanter by the side of the fire,

when a large number of guests circled round the winter's hearth—stood with the candles, one close to Mrs. Carden, the other near Martha, on the chair next to her. Mrs. Carden never nodded her head, nor ceased to glare at Martha through her spectacles. She scarcely required even an occasional glance at her knitting.

Martha thought of the sleepless bride, who drove her husband mad by the unwinking constancy of her gaze night and day. She grew more and more confused in her ideas, and attached no meaning to the sentences through which she stumbled.

The hour of release came at length—half-past nine. Then Mrs. Carden rang the bell, when a cook and kitchen-maid, with Ruth, joined the prayers read by their mistress in an audible voice. It seemed to strike Mrs. Carden that she had not offered tea to her guests; and she apologised, saying that she had forgotten it, not taking it herself.

'How quiet everything is here!' whispered Mrs. Clemens as they retired to their room, which was at the back of the house. 'I declare 'twould be a comfort to hear the spray of the sea splashing up against the garden-wall at home. I wonder what kind of place there is outside;' and she removed the heavy curtains, and opening the window-shutters, looked out on the garden, dark with the gloom of a night in February. 'Perhaps it may not be so lonesome to-morrow,' added the widow; and Martha sighed an incredulous assent.

''Tis very cold; there is frost in the air.'

''Tis much colder than Cornwall,' said Mrs. Clemens. 'They say these eastern counties are colder. 'Tis a beautiful soft bed, though, Martha dear; and I do declare if there ain't a frill all round the pillow-case!—a wonderful trouble to get up in the ironing. I wonder what time Betsy breakfasts.'

CHAPTER IX.

' There stood a clock—though small the owner's need,
For habit told how all things should proceed.
Fix'd were their habits, and they rose betimes,
Then pray'd their hour, and sang their early rhymes.'

CRABBE.

RUTH knocked at the door at half-past seven next morning with hot water. Martha had locked it before she placed herself by her mother's side, from the feeling of insecurity sometimes experienced in a strange house. Ruth awaited her opening it grimly, with the information that breakfast would be ready at five minutes past eight o'clock, and that prayers would be read when the clock should strike.

Martha awoke her mother from an unpleasant excursion in dreamland—where she saw Martha, dressed as a bride, at the altar, whilst her wedding dress and veil suddenly turned into grave-clothes —and told her the orders for breakfast.

'Well, my dear, 'tis a comfort to have the water brought hot instead of having to light the fire and heat it.'

'Do you think so, mother? I had rather do all the work myself, and clean up the kitchen, than live in this dreadful thraldom.'

'Well, my dear, we must make the best of it;' and with that wise determination they dressed and went downstairs.

Mrs. Carden was awaiting them when they descended; and preceded them to the dining-room, where she read prayers. She hoped they had rested well, in a formal manner; and on having received their assurances to that effect, they partook of a frugal breakfast of weak coffee and dry toast. There were three pieces in a handsome silver rack; and when each person had received their share, and drank their coffee, the breakfast was concluded.

'You will read the collect for the day, the psalms and lessons, niece,' said their hostess, addressing Martha.

'I read badly, aunt. I think you must have had enough of that last night.'

'You read badly! 'Tis to be hoped you will improve. Probably your parents did not attend to your education.'

'I declare,' said poor Mrs. Clemens, 'Martha had thirteen quarters, all paid for, and extras for two quarters, when my poor dear husband died, and I could not continue it; but she know'd how to keep the pot boiling for her old mother by needlework; and as to accomplishments, she've done the beautifulest cover for what they call an automaton to sit on that anybody ever see'd. I didn't need to ask you for a sixpence, Betsy, though you was my own flesh and blood; and if you don't find your goddaughter so clever at reading as you could wish, you might have given us a little help sooner. A girl is full old to learn new ways of speaking and reading at twenty-seven years.'

There was a great deal of unpleasant truth in Mrs. Clemens' observations, which admitted of no legitimate response. So Mrs. Carden made none, but merely asked Martha in an aggressive tone if she meant to oblige her or not; and as this was accompanied by the offer of the prayer-book, Martha took it, and read the service of the day better than she had performed Mr. Smallridge's milk-and-water discourses on the previous night.

The mother and daughter perceived that they would be expected to conform to the worship used by the Church of England; and as Mrs. Clemens had no quarrel with any of the church-goers in Lynn touching hassocks, and as the Methodists do not object to Church of England service, they had no objection to conform to its ritual.

The reading concluded as the melancholy clock chimed eleven.

'Nancy, have you nothing to employ your fingers?' said Mrs. Carden.

'No, sister; I have no company-work; only stockings to mend.'

'What on earth do you do with yourself all day when you are at home? You can't always be mending stockings.'

'There's plenty to do, sister; as you would find, if you had to scrub and scour and clean as I did. Look at my hands; they don't look as if I had passed my life in doing nothing.'

'*My* sister can't do the work of a kitchen-maid here. Do you think you could knit like this?' holding out a square of well-executed knitting.

'Yes; if I had the cotton and pins.'

'I will give you some to keep you employed.'

'Well, sister, I'll do my best in a plain way; and if I hold my cotton looser than you, which is likely, you must tell me in time.'

'Aunt, if you will give me some red sewing-silk, I will darn the damask curtains in the room in which we sleep,' proposed Martha, who felt stifled in her aunt's presence, and would have given much to escape, even into the freezing atmosphere of the fireless bedroom.

Mrs. Carden arose slowly, and taking a great needle-book from a massive silk bag, placed it in Martha's hands, telling her that it contained skeins of different-coloured silk, from which she might select that which would agree best with the curtains. With these materials she retreated, leaving the sisters together—a wise proceeding, as confidential intercourse was more likely to result from the absence of a third person.

The beginning was not, however, propitious.

'Betsy,' said Mrs. Clemens, 'now I've got accustomed to the alteration, I don't think you are looking in bad health.'

In truth, Mrs. Clemens had expected the importance of being a sick-nurse; and was somewhat disappointed at finding no occupation which would call her into a position of dignity in the house. She had expected to be moving on tiptoe round a sick-bed, or making some delectable beef-tea, or receiving instructions from a doctor as to drops and draught so many times in the day and night.

'Are you disappointed not to find me dying, Nancy?'

'Dear, dear! what a dreadful thing to fancy, sister! No, of course not. 'Tis a great pleasure to see you so well, and so comfortably off—so healthy and wealthy and wise—I s'pose 'tis 'cause you get up so early; not but that I've always got up betimes myself; and I never was wealthy, nor wise for the matter of that.'

'I cannot say that I am wise,' said Mrs. Carden; 'but I am as wealthy and as healthy as a woman can be who carries about with her a disease that reminds her hourly that death is coming, and will not be evaded. Listen, Nancy: there was a

famous warrior and emperor who had a shroud
carried before him like a banner, with this inscription, "Thou shalt die." Now, that I have impressed
on me night and day without intermission or re-
mission by different degrees of pain.'

'Lor, Betsy, don't talk so dreadfully. Why
don't you go to a doctor and get cured?' said Mrs.
Clemens, some bygone sisterly tenderness returning, as she heard this confession of hitherto-con-
cealed suffering.

The nearest approach to a smile which Nancy
had as yet seen made a faint ripple over the hard
handsome face of the younger sister.

'Doctors are good for things they are really
wanted for. If I broke a leg or an arm, I should
send for one; but when it comes to a complaint
like mine, I know there is no cure; and I won't
have any jackanapes sending me his nasty physic
and his long bill for nothing. If there is anything
really wrong, no doctor can cure you; if there is
not, you'll get well without one.'

'O, Betsy, if I was you, I'd go to London, and
have the best advice the world could give me; I
would not go out of life without trying to live
longer. Surely life is sweet; and 'tis pleasant
to "behold the face of the sun," as Job says;

though I must say one don't see it often this weather.'

'Yes, life is sweet,' said Mrs. Carden, softened by seeing the earnest tears starting in Nancy's eyes; 'and I would live longer if I could; but

> 'Why, Father, shrink from Thy decree,
> If so my trembling soul be led
> A shorter, safer way to Thee?'

And Mrs. Carden's stern face became beautiful with an expression of resignation. A spring may be choked up by rubbish, broken walls, mossy stones, decaying leaves, and branches of trees, and remain unvisited, and losing its utility and beauty in an oozing marsh; but let some chance circumstance remove its incumbrances,

> 'with a gentle leap
> The rill runs o'er; around, wild ferns and ivy creep,
> Fantastically tangled.'

Thus was it with the sisterly affection which had slumbered so long under the accumulated power of circumstances and absence.

A thousand recollections of home-life rushed on the muddled brains of the elder sister, and softened her heart to one so recently refound, and so inevitably death-doomed.

She sat looking tenderly at Mrs. Carden,

whose thought had wandered into that dim futurity whose paths she must so soon tread alone—

> ' Where none weigh'd out silver nor counted gold,
> Nothing was bought and nothing sold ;
> None would give and none would take ;
> No one answer'd, no one spake ;
> Poverty was not, nor any wealth ;
> None knew sickness and none knew health.'

' O, sister Betsy,' she said, ' do you remember how fond we were of each other when we were small things, when mother died, and we went to live with grandmother? Ah, she was father's mother; mother's mother would have been more tender like. Grandmothers on the mother's side mostly are.'

' Yes, I remember,' said Mrs. Carden ; ' but I was three years younger than you, so it isn't so plain to my memory.'

' Well, we played together hide-and-seek, and when we cried whoop, grandmother called us good-for-nothing hussies for making a noise, and she sent me every day to the school next door, to keep me quiet, she said. The two gardens joined. I had to sit for hours on a hard form till my back ached. One day I was sure I heard your little voice crying and calling, "Nancy," so I slipped out into the garden when the mistress was unpicking a letter in a sampler that a girl had done wrong, so that she didn't see me; and there I saw a little fat hand and arm pushed through the palings of the fence, all bleeding from the thorns of a gooseberry-bush, and your beautiful golden hair was tangled in its branches. Tears were running down your pretty cheeks, and you cried, "Nancy, Nancy, come back to me!" I could not get through the hedge to you, and only your little arm could reach to me; so we cried together till the mistress on one side, and grandmother on the other, came and dragged us away. Grandmother put her hard skinny hand down your back, and caught hold of the little body of your frock, and tore you away, leaving your hair on the bushes. I heard you screech, and I screeched for company, and missus gave me a box in the ear and kept me in half-an-hour sitting in a corner when the other girls were gone, and I knew you were fretting for me all the time.'

'I only remember that in a kind of dream,' said Mrs. Carden; 'but I do recollect, when I was a girl of nine or ten, how I went out blackberry-ing; and after I had eaten as much as I could, I wanted to bring some fine ones home for you. I had a new white-calico bonnet on, all drawn through

with cottons; and I put some leaves in the head of
the bonnet and filled it with blackberries. Then,
thinking grandmother would scold 'cause it was
so late, I ran all the way home, and when I got to
the garden-gate I looked down, and, good lawk!
the juice of the nasty things had all run out, and
dyed the caul of the bonnet deep red. Grandmother saw me coming, and opened the door to
scold at my being so late. "Where's your bonnet?" said she. "Here in my hand," said I, quite
careless like, with my hand down at my side, just
letting her see the poke, and the white strings that
I held it by. "Go up, you good-for-nothing girl,
and wash your hands for tea, and put away your
bonnet carefully," said she. Up I went, as white
as a sheet, and the caul of the bonnet was full of
mashed seeds, and the juice dropping all over the
floor.'

'Yes,' said Mrs. Clemens; 'I remember how
I put the bonnet in water, and first the nasty thing
turned purple, and as I put plenty of soap it looked
blue, and not a bit would it budge from that.
When grandmother went to bed, I stole out, and
begged Miss Botterel to make another directly,
before it was found out.'

'Yes, Nancy; you paid four shillings and sixpence out of your own money that I might not be beaten. You always was lavish of your money,' she added reproachfully.

'Well, my dear, 'twas well bestowed if it saved your dear shoulders from the rod. O, how that old woman did lay it on!'

'Yes, she did,' said Mrs. Carden meditatively; 'but 'twas hard on her to have two troublesome children to maintain, when she had brought up all her own and got them off her hands. And father was very aggravating to go marrying again.'

'I don't approve of second marriages,' said the elder matron. 'Nothing could ever have tempted *me* to forget my dear old man.'

Mrs. Clemens did not recollect that, when her husband had met his death, she had had three grown-up children, and was deficient in those incitements to matrimony in the opposite sex—youth, bloom, and money. Who would have been tempted to make a woman break her vow of constancy to a dead husband, when her beauty and wealth had vanished? It had been difficult enough to find a suitor for her daughter.

'Umph!' said Mrs. Carden, 'I am not clear that I agree with you; but it don't matter.'

CHAPTER X.

'Twelve months her sables she in sorrow wore,
And mourn'd so long that she could mourn no more.'

CRABBE.

MRS. CARDEN had good reasons for not agree-
ing with her sister's condemnation of second marriages. She had been united to an old man for
his money, and had not lived unhappily with him,
considering the difference of age. He had existed
to the uttermost verge of human life, and when he
died, Mrs. Carden was considered an elderly woman; but having been younger than her husband
so many years, she could not help judging herself by his measurement, and feeling that she was
youthful, forgetting that she was so only as compared to him.

Mrs. Carden's manager was a man of forty,
well-looking and alert. If the widow regarded
him with favourable eyes, it was not to be wondered at; considering that he was attractive and
manly in aspect, and regular in conduct, besides
being indispensable to her in conducting such portions of her husband's business as were too lucra-
tive to be given up at his death.

For the last fifteen years of Mr. Carden's life, the masculine intellect of Mrs. Carden had taken the place of her husband's weakened mind in the conduct of the business. She decided on what courses should be adopted, and Mr. Marchbanks the manager carried out her intentions without resenting the sway of an intellect of which the results were the increasing capital of the business. Both the woman and her agent loved success, and they loved the money they accumulated. Possibly when Mr. Carden died, this love of pelf, and the intimate union of similar interests in business, might have led to one still more intimate; but when money had not been the all-absorbing passion of Harold Marchbanks, he had engaged himself to be married to a respectable young woman, and had kept their love a secret till such time as his increased income should admit of their union.

If he suspected the existence of any intention too flattering to his vanity in the widow, he at any event had the honesty, so soon as he was made a partner in the firm of Carden and Marchbanks, timber-merchants, to inform Mrs. Carden that he was furnishing a house for the young woman whom he had chosen for his wife.

If Mrs. Carden was mortified, she did not show it, nor did she ever display the slightest vexation in her manner towards him. She was sorry, because it would have been a convenient arrangement, and would have kept the money well together; but she was fond of power, and perhaps was consoled for her disappointment by a little doubt whether the manager might not, when merged in the husband, have proved less tractable than the deceased Mr. Carden.

The bloom had faded from Mary Brooks' cheek when she stood before the altar with Harold Marchbanks. She had waited for years, and had seen another love take possession of the heart which had been wholly hers; but the rival was 'the vile yellow slave' of Leyden the poet; and women put up with a devotion of which the object is unconscious and inanimate, and of which they ultimately reap the advantage.

Spiteful people said she had waited too long, especially when they saw the wealth displayed in the furniture of the new house, and the beauty of all its appointments. If she had waited, she had the advantage of inhabiting what seemed to her a palace in its magnificence and luxury.

In the mean time, symptoms that she was mortal impressed themselves on, and took possession of, Mrs. Carden's mind; and not feeling inclined to endow Mrs. Marchbanks or her issue with her wealth, from a little leaven of feminine mortification, she turned her thoughts to her impoverished sister and her forgotten goddaughter. Nancy had always been tender to her, though somewhat of a fool, she remembered. Of Martha she knew of course nothing, but that she was of her own flesh and blood. She knew that she herself must die either sooner or later, and she wished that the gold she had loved so devotedly during many years of her life should be cared for and kept together at her death.

When Martha had read badly, stupidly, in fact, she felt irritated against her; but when Mrs. Clemens had suggested that a little aid in her education might have rectified that of which she complained, she was conscience-stricken by the truth of the reproach, and inclined to be more tolerant of a defect which a little more liberality on her part might have rectified. She might reproach herself; but the vulgar proverb, that silk purses are not made out of sows' ears, would have applied to Martha. She was by nature slow, and not easily sensible to mental influences. Once impressed, however, the marks were indelible. She was not like the plume on the warrior's casque, moving with every breath of the summer air, but the casque itself, which, once dinted, retains the marks for ever, notwithstanding the efforts of the skilful henchman to polish them away. Or she was like the logging stone, which was moved with an effort for some time, but once touched by a reckless impetus is for ever motionless.

When the trio met for luncheon, Martha had pretty well exhausted the crimson sewing-silk, and Mrs. Carden said that they would get some when they went out in the carriage.

'I always drive out at two o'clock,' she said, 'and you, Nancy will accompany me. I prefer one person at a time. I will take Martha to-morrow, if she pleases.'

Mrs. Clemens, though she was eager for the honour of being conveyed about in her sister's carriage, wished Martha to enjoy that satisfaction, and was about to propose it, when her daughter said curtly,

'Thank you, aunt, but I do not like carriage exercise; if my mother does, you had better take her every day. It makes me ill, and I much prefer walking.'

This did not sound very gracious, and Mrs. Carden thought that her goddaughter was a very independent young woman; the more so as when the carriage came round, Martha, with her bonnet and cloak on, passed it on an outward-bound expedition to see the town and its outskirts. She fancied she could not breathe in the gloomy rooms with their heavy silk curtains, and stepped lightly over the crisp frosty ground, across the large market-place, till she came to the fine old avenue which led by the ruined building, where pilgrims had been wont to find a night's shelter, when the closed gates prevented their seeking hospitality in the town. She looked at this relic of the past with interest, for these wanderers had been Catholics, and with interest did she contemplate the venerable tower of the Gray Friars. Her Philip had been educated in a convent, and she felt disposed to love all Catholics for his sake.

She scarcely knew why she felt so antagonistic to her aunt. Her mother seemed to like her, and to be reconciling herself to her Lynn life, and Martha felt that she could never do so. She had rather be back working herself blind for her mother than live with this cold-hearted relative. She saw, too, that she should never be permitted to earn any money there by dress-making; her aunt's niece could never be permitted thus to degrade her rich relative. How could she save any money in this way to give to her Philip, or to provide for their future housekeeping? It was all wretched for her, she thought; and she was jealous of the love with which her mother seemed to regard Mrs. Carden. She liked to earn money; she had been accustomed to do so ever since she had left school; she had worked to support her mother; she not unnaturally, now that the strain put on her by want was relaxed, wished to earn some for herself. What comfort was it to have a mutton-chop for dinner, in the place of mealy potatoes and a salt herring as a treat, when she was obliged to read, which she had not been accustomed to do; and was expected to be grateful for exemption from labour, which, though she had grumbled at its intensity, she now thought infinitely preferable to Smallridge's sermons?

'O, that weary book!' said the poor girl, stamping her feet on the hard ground; 'are we to have it again to-night?'

She looked along the flat waveless river, with its black vessels lying at the slumbrous quay, where frost seemed to have paralysed industry, holding the stiffened sails with strenuous grasp, and deadening enterprise. Mists hung over the distant horizon, from whence the wild sea-birds flew circling with shrill cries towards the land, driven thither by the unusual cold. Martha longed for the dashing waves of the Cornish coast and its dark rugged rocks; though the thought of the prediction uttered as to her fate filled her with melancholy.

'He is but a mad boy,' she said; 'and though I was fearful to embark, no accident happened to me. Why should I fear? I must go back; my mother may miss me, if she be returned. But no, she is too much taken up with this woman, who left us to live or die for twenty years without even giving her sister a guinea to buy a mourning dress for her husband, or a bit of bread for her breakfast.'

Martha was a little comforted by seeing her mother's face, pale with anxiety, pressed against the drawing-room window which looked into the square, as she ascended the flight of stone steps which led to the door. Her aunt was not in the room to remonstrate with and reprove Mrs. Clemens for her absurd anxiety, which was by no means unreasonable, seeing that Martha had never been in Lynn before, and might have lost her way, or

otherwise have got into difficulties.   She saw not,
and therefore could not disapprove, the tender
caress given by that admiring mother to the cheek
tinted to a delicate pink colour by exercise.

'O, Martha, *where* have you been so long, my
dear?   I was watching out of the carriage window
all the way I went, and could not listen to anything sister Betsy said to me, because I was so
afraid something might happen to you.   And
when the carriage drove up to the door, and Ruth
opened it, says I, "Is Miss Clemens come back?"
and my heart was up in my mouth to hear her
answer; and thought I, "She'd be watching for the
carriage to bring me back if she had come home;"
and lor', when she said no, I turned so sick at
heart that I trembled all over, and could hardly
get up those weary steps.'

'Well, mother, if you are anxious, I won't go
out again; I've seen enough of the ugly place; in
future I had just as soon walk in the garden.'

Mrs. Carden came in at that moment, and
recommended Martha to take off her bonnet and
cloak, 'as people should when they come into a
house; and in future, remember to rub your shoes,
and keep a pair downstairs in that well in the
window-seat of the hall, that you may not carry

upstairs any of the dust or gravel which may cling to your feet.'

' 'Tis a hard frost, and as dry as a bone, aunt; so I am sure my shoes cannot have hurt your carpet,' said Martha.

' If you consider,' said Mrs. Carden, 'what mingled pollutions your feet *must* have passed over even before you had crossed the market-place, you must perceive that the shoes which have been in contact with such cannot be fit to place upon a substance not intended to be washed.'

Martha, to use an expressive phrase, flounced out of the room; by which is indicated a peculiar exhibition of irritability in the walk, which flings the petticoats into the shape of a succession of loops. As in the year 1827 they were not very full, these indications were more evident.

'Your daughter has not a good temper, Nancy,' said Mrs. Carden.

' O, sister, how can you say so !' replied the mother. 'Martha has the sweetest disposition I ever met.'

'Umph ! you must have been unfortunate in your associates if this is really the case,' rejoined the aunt. But Mrs. Clemens did not catch the innuendo, and passed it over in silence.

Semi-deaf people often turn away wrath, not by a soft answer, but none at all. 'I daresay 'tis something unpleasant,' is the feeling of these long-sufferers, ' so I won't ask them to repeat it.'

Whilst Martha lingered in her room, unwilling to return to that which contained her aunt, Mrs. Carden entered with the red sewing-silk. She took up the mended curtain, and examined it curiously through her spectacles; then dropped it without the word of commendation which it deserved.

Martha knew that no one could have done it better, and did not care for her aunt's silence, though she disliked her the more on account of it.

'There is no more light to sew by; you had better come downstairs,' said the peremptory lady. So Martha came down, having provided herself with a work-bag, in the hope that her occupation might exonerate her from reading. There was nothing to be done, however, but sit still in the February twilight; and for once Martha was glad of the absence of candles—she would be expected to read again when they were lighted. She sat silent, and thought of Philip; and pressed her ringed hand to the locket which lay concealed on her breast. She thought of the caress which he had given the top of her head when he first showed her the portrait; and her dull heart glowed with concealed passion for her beloved, who was not, alas, her lover. As she pondered on the past, there was a gentle ring at the front door, which, softly as it tingled, made Mrs. Carden start. No one spoke: Martha, because she was indifferent—the sound said nothing to her; Mrs. Carden, because she held her breath to listen for a step; Mrs. Clemens, because, being rather deaf, the peal had been inaudible to her.

A minute after, Ruth announced Mr. Marchbanks, who entered, bowing to the mistress of the house, including in the sweep of his salutation the two strange ladies.

CHAPTER XI.

'The wealth her husband left, her care retain'd.'
                                    CRABBE.

'I HAVE come, madam, to know your wishes on certain matters which require decision before the post goes out. You will allow me to ring for candles,' he said, pulling the bell without waiting for permission, 'for there is no time to lose.'

Mrs. Carden was affronted by what she conceived to be a liberty taken, and by the necessity to hurry imposed on herself.

'I should have thought,' said she magisterially, 'that you would have given me more time to consider the subject. I am not accustomed to decide on matters of importance at a moment's notice.'

Mr. Marchbanks was about to say that he had turned the subject over in his mind already; but as he knew that would only aggravate the offence, he was silent. He seated himself in one of the chairs against the wall till Ruth appeared with the tall silver candlesticks, and placed them on the small table before her mistress. Martha looked up with some curiosity to see if Mr. Marchbanks would venture to move his chair from its place; but he rose and knelt by the little table, taking from the side-pocket of his coat several letters, which Mrs. Carden, wiping her spectacles deliberately, perused attentively. Some brief questions, unintelligible to the mother and daughter, having been asked by the lady and answered by the manager, she wrote her orders on the outside of each communication, and gave them back to him. Martha observed that his hand shook as he took them, refolding and putting them in his pocket-book; then rising hastily, and repeating his bow to the circle, he rushed from the house, saying apologetically that he was fearful the answers would be too late for the post.

'Dear, dear,' said Mrs. Clemens as the door closed after him, 'what a nice-looking gentleman! So neat, and such a clean shirt-collar! and I declare the frill in front of his shirt must have cost eighteen shillings a yard, if a penny; and very well got-up too. Poor gentleman!'

'Why *poor* gentleman,' said Mrs. Carden shortly, 'when everything you said before goes to prove that he is a rich one?'

'O, well, sister,' responded the elder woman timidly, 'perhaps I am wrong; but there was a look of trouble on his poor face that made my heart ache.'

'Was there?' asked, or rather exclaimed, the sister, her suspicions pointing to possible losses in mercantile affairs.

'Yes, sister, I think so. His eyelids were so swollen, that he looked as if he had been up all night, for all his being so spruce and brushed up so neat.'

This was quite enough to make Mrs. Carden thoughtful. Could he have heard anything of the loss of the last consignment of timber from Norway, about which he had expressed some anxiety? and had he been purposely silent before the two strangers?

She went upstairs when the half-hour bell rang previous to dinner, and stood silently considering what the disturbance in Mr. Marchbanks' face could mean, which had been sufficiently indicated to attract the notice of a person so unobservant as her sister, when Ruth, who was pouring warm water into the washing-basin, said:

'Did Mr. Marchbanks say how he left his lady, ma'am?'

'His *lady*?' said her mistress contemptuously. 'Do you mean Polly Brooks that was?'

'Yes; Mrs. Marchbanks. They say she has been very bad two days and two nights, and the child is not born, and they don't expect she will *continie.*'

'No; I did not ask. How could I know? Send up Sally by and by, and hear how she is, with my compliments.'

'I wonder why he did not tell me?' said she to herself, guiltily suspecting that, from some, she hoped, undefined feeling in his mind, he knew that she would not care for the cause of his present distress.

This had been the case. With all the anxieties of a husband and a possible father on his mind, he felt as if he could not speak of them to a woman who would be so utterly unsympathetic.

Mrs. Carden, when she had washed her hands, met her relatives in the drawing-room with a mind relieved from apprehension; so much easier is it to contemplate a misfortune that affects our friends only than one in which we are ourselves complicated. No doubt it was very sad that the manager should lose his wife of twelve months' standing; but that was his affair only. Had the vessel been wrecked in those wintry storms in the Baltic, both he and she would have been serious losers.

' Of course,' she said, thinking the matter over, ' there was great risk in Polly Brooks marrying when she was more than forty. I daresay she will die in childbirth. She might have expected it. That comes of waiting so long!' forgetting that, had the unfortunate couple married fifteen years before, she would have been the first person to condemn their imprudence.

That evening Martha produced her work from a large bag, and seated herself as near the candles as she could. Mrs. Carden did not consequently ask her to read; but, as Mrs. Clemens was slowly adding one stitch to another in her knitting, and begging Martha to rectify her mistakes when she dropped one, Mrs. Carden said she would read to them an interesting account of one of her husband's ancestors, of whose memory Mr. Carden had been very proud.

'CHAPTER XII.

' O Truth, our homage must be thine :
    When perfect, we thy form discern ;
    But clouds around thy brow divine
    Have cast a shadow stern.'

IN the year of our Lord 1547, a young man belonging to Lynn by birth and connections, named Silas Carden, had been sent on some matter of business to the house of his uncle at Coxall in Essex. This uncle had embraced the reformed religion, and diligently strove that the light which shone on him should reflect its rays on the benighted soul of his nephew. Silas, though shaken in his faith, still clung to it with the timidity of reverence and early devotion; for his parents were Catholics.

Whilst his mind thus wavered, his uncle confided to him an intention which, if carried out, would be believed, and tend to consolidate the conviction of which he had striven to lay the foundation. Silas had spoken of the constant miracles performed by the idol called the Rood at Dovercourt. The touch of this image did make the blind to see, and the lame to walk; whilst

those sick of divers diseases, if laid before its
shrine, were straightway healed of their infirmities. One woman who had been unable, as she
stated, to move from her bed for eight years,
whose dwelling being nigh unto that of his father
he had known of her feeble condition, had been
carried by men's hands on a litter to the church
in which the idol was enshrined, and after the
priest had offered up many and fervent supplica-
tions, her vigour had been restored to her, and
she had risen from her bed, singing and praising
God, who had given such power to the Church
to ameliorate the condition of His servants.

Mr. Reuben Carden averred that the woman
so cured had acted under delusion, being wrought
on by a lively imagination, or had committed a
deliberate imposture; and he asked of his nephew
whether he believed that an image possessed of
such marvellous virtue would not be able to strike
with signal punishment any sacrilegious hand that
should violate the sanctity of its shrine.

Silas replied that, as he believed it was truly
endowed with miraculous power, so he also believed
that it would inflict divers penalties and sundry
kinds of death on any one who should outrage
even the sacred building which contained it.

'Then,' said Reuben Carden, 'behold, two others have joined themselves unto me in this work—holy men, whose hearts are grieved for the backslidings and abominations of Israel. Thou shalt go with these brethren and judge the result.'

Then one night they set out, taking with them the youth Silas Carden; and when they had reached a certain spot, they collected a goodly pile of wood from a farmer's yard, leaving the money in an earthen vessel to pay for the same. It was a fair twilight when they started, in the month of January, and the frost was crisp to their feet; but presently the sky clouded over, and a mighty rushing wind arose, which, howling dismally over the common, with the dread of what his companions might mean, filled the soul of the young man with terror.

At length they reached the church at Dovercourt, which, behold, did stand right open; for so it was believed was the will of the saint whose image was there worshipped, and those who bowed down to him did aver that no mortal strength availed to close the doors of this edifice.

When Reuben Carden drew near to the church, Silas flung himself on his knees before his uncle and clung obstinately to his feet, saying:

'Do not this great sin, my uncle, lest the vengeance of St. Barnabas overtake thee!'

And his uncle answering, said:

'Come on in peace; for no harm shall reach unto thee or me.'

So they entered the church, and there stood the image accounted holy, in a shrine, with four tapers burning before it. The saint, seen in a halo of light through the night mist that filled the temple, shone stern and awful as he seemed to glare at the intruders.

Then the heart of Silas failed him with fear; but his uncle exclaimed:

'See there, how the idol is adorned with a cloven cap on his head, which is called a mitre. In Nineveh of the Gentiles they thus adorned their fish-god Dagon. The cloven cap represented the open jaw of the fish, the scaly skin flowed down on Dagon behind, even as the robe of this profane idol. The precious stones even have imitated the eyes of the fish. This idolatry the backsliding Israelites fell into when in captivity in Babylon; and we, children of the truth, worshipping Christ in simplicity and purity, are tempted by this, a lying image, into the sins which brought judgments unto that stiff-necked people. Up, brethren! let us cast down this impudent impostor. Let him lie, even as lay his prototype Dagon, on his face, with his arms extended, broken and helpless; let us bear him to the fire which will consume him, that he may no longer cause those who worship him to be consumed in everlasting flames.'

Thus saying, Reuben Carden flung a rope, which he had brought coiled under his cloak; and his friends joining their strength with his, they dragged the image from its shrine.

Silas watched that they should be paralysed into helplessness, or that a flash of lightning from heaven should strike them blind; but there was no sign of disapprobation from on high. The cold moon gleamed through the broken masses of clouds hurrying over her through the high arched windows, contrasting her pale beams with the glare of the tall tapers. Nature seemed indifferent to the sacrilege committed.

The men dragged the idol over the rugged ground, which was covered with shreds of its glittering adornments, as the brambles caught the folds of its robes. The men proceeded in silence, Silas bearing the wax-lights extinguished by the blast, till they came to the waste ground where they had made a kind of funeral pile. Thereon they placed the image, and the tapers around it; and Reuben Carden, striking a light from the tinder-box he had provided, set fire to the candles and to the pyre, which flamed up, and lighted the sky above it with an angry glow. But the men proceeded on their way triumphantly, turning round often to see the goodly blaze, which was visible for more than a mile on their journey.

During Mrs. Carden's reading, Ruth came to the door; but on a sign from her mistress she sat down on the nearest chair, and awaited the conclusion. When Mrs. Carden had placed the mark carefully between the leaves of the small pamphlet, she looked up, and said:

'Well?'

'If you please, ma'am, Mrs. Marchbanks is no better.'

'Umph!' said the lady.

There was a pause.

'Ah! that poor gentleman's wife or mother is ill, then. I thought he was in trouble; I said so, you remember, Betsy.'

No one noticed Mrs. Clemens' little triumph of superior penetration, and Ruth went on:

'They've sent to London for some great man

amongst the doctors; but if Mr. Marchbanks had done what was right, they say he'd have sent before now.'

'A pack of nonsense! If she's to live, she'll live; and if she's to die, she'll die, and no doctors can save her!' said the mistress.

'That's as the Lord may will,' said the servant. 'Nothing more, ma'am?'

'No, you may go.'

Mrs. Clemens was full of curiosity and anxiety about Mrs. Marchbanks. She had a mind which interested itself in small objects, thus finding nourishment like the ass on the barest of commons.

Mrs. Carden answered her briefly. Mr. Marchbanks had been first her husband's clerk, then manager, and was now partner in the firm with herself. He had married a woman over forty, and this danger was the result.

On the following day nothing was heard from Mr. Marchbanks. The frost increased in intensity, and Mrs. Carden declined to have her horses roughed, or to go out in the carriage without this precaution.

Martha walked under the platforms of melancholy cedars in the garden, and gazed on the clustered chrysanthemums hanging their frosted heads, without seeing them. Something she did see—a bit of warm colour lying on the fibres of the cedars. As she looked at it, there was a little tremulous movement in one of the fibres, she thought. She stooped, and found that the convulsive jerk had proceeded from a robin's leg, dying or dead from the cold. She took the bird up tenderly and laid it on her bosom, striving to warm it back into life. She walked faster to add to the circulation of her blood, and thus increased the glow within its resting-place. She connected the fate of this little creature, the victim to the inclemency of the air, with that of the youth whom the tempest had flung at her feet—each had depended on her for his chance of life. She had saved Philip, and had been repaid by the love she had lavished—payment almost sufficient for a loving woman. With all the aching of her jealous heart, she would not have been without the devotion to Philip which had occasioned this suffering.

And this small bird seemed sent by Providence to make her residence with her aunt tolerable to her. She would shelter the little creature in their bedroom, and let it fly out when the weather was warmer. Martha was happier than she had been since she heard the tramp of the pale horse carry-ing off the man she so loved.

In the room occupied by her mother and her-self was a large wicker basket, like those in which dress - makers carry their delicate fabrications, which was lined with faded pink calico, and had been placed in the room to conceal from dust the bonnets of the guests. When the bird began to move the white film of his eyelids, and afterwards to rebel against the breast that had restored it to life by little angry flutterings, Martha returned to the house and placed him in the wicker retreat, a solitary monk in an untenanted cloister. There, after luncheon, she fed him with crumbs from bits of bread concealed surreptitiously from prying eyes; not without some anxiety lest his super-fluous activity should reveal him to Ruth when she came to turn the beds down in the evening, alarmed as he might be into indiscreet flutterings.

Her next thought was to provide a perch for his comfort, and for this she returned to the gar-den, and cut down the straight branch of a lilac-tree. When trimmed, the twig was placed across the basket, and its two extremities protruded about half an inch on each side through holes which, I grieve to say, Martha had made in the lining.

CHAPTER XIII.

'Kindness by secret sympathy is tied,
  For noble souls by nature are allied.'
                                        DRYDEN.

A RING came at the door just as Mrs. Carden
had gone to her room to prepare for dinner. Martha was with her bird, and Mrs. Clemens alone
in the sitting-room, when Mr. Marchbanks walked
in, looking more wan than ever.

Mrs. Clemens arose. With her face quivering
with sympathy and her anxious eyes fixed on the
new-comer, she stammered out,

'Is she—is she better?'

Mr. Marchbanks had nerved himself to answer the formal inquiry from Mrs. Carden he
expected after the message of the previous evening; but he had not prepared himself for the
genuine emotion shown by this tender-hearted
woman, and his voice broke into a sob as he
turned away his face, and said,

'Yes, she is better, thank God, for she can
never suffer more. She is dead.'

He sat down, and Mrs. Clemens seated herself

by him, with tears running down her withered cheeks.

'It is God's will,' she said.

'No, madam, not that. It was— She might have been saved, they said, if I had sent to London sooner. But it was that vile care of money—'

He sat upright suddenly, and took some papers from his pocket-book. His quick ear had detected the sound of his partner's step on the stairs. His face, though wan, was schooled into tranquillity in a moment of time.

He rose and bowed as Mrs. Carden entered; and as she shaped her query in the hope that he could give a better account of Mrs. Marchbanks, he replied in a measured tone, 'She died at half-past three o'clock, madam;' and then began to speak on the business which was too urgent to admit of his giving the early hours of his loss to solitary grief.

'I am sorry,' said Mrs. Carden, 'for your trouble;' and went on to express her wishes as to each letter as she read them, without any farther reference to his loss.

'Has the Lily of Lynn been sighted yet?' she said.

'No, madam. I went to the top of the Gray

Friars tower at noon to-day; but she had not appeared yet on the horizon to be visible through my spy-glass, which is a powerful one. The monks left us a valuable legacy in that edifice,' he observed.

''Twas well,' replied the lady, 'that they should serve some good purpose, as they caused so much sorrow and harboured so many evil-doers. It was a monk of the Gray Friars who denounced my husband's ancestor, and stood by his funeral pile when he bore witness to the truth by his martyrdom.'

'So I have heard my late principal say,' replied Mr. Marchbanks, with the air of not knowing what he expressed.

He departed as soon as he could, glad to escape to the accordant gloom of his silent and deserted home.

'Dear heart! Poor man,' said Mrs. Clemens, 'how I do feel for him, to be sure! 'Tis hard to think that she is gone; but far worse to believe that he might have saved her and didn't, all along of money. I wish I'd asked about the baby.'

'What can you mean?' asked the sister in astonishment; 'and what can you know about it?'

'Only what he said to me, my dear,' replied

Mrs. Clemens, looking rather frightened at having betrayed her conversation with the stranger.

'I cannot imagine,' said Mrs. Carden stiffly, 'about what you could have spoken to him at all.'

Mrs. Clemens, who was rather deaf, did not understand this, and therefore made no response; a circumstance which added to her offences in the opinion of her sister, who was thus left in ignorance of anything that had passed. She did not choose to insist on Nancy's telling her, and was too proud to inquire farther.

Mrs. Carden seemed to think that she was entitled to a monopoly of all the conversation which took place in her house, and felt jealous that any one else should know any circumstance or utter any sentiment to her unknown.

That evening she continued the narrative of Silas Carden.

CHAPTER XIV.

'The fortitude of patience and heroic martyrdom.'
MILTON.

WHEN the loss of the holy Rood of Dovercourt was first known, it was conjectured that some pious men, jealous of the reputation belonging to the church which contained an image of such sanctity, had carried it off, to place it in some cathedral of their own. It was even supposed by some more credulous, that the saint had himself chosen to seek another domicile, and, in preparation for such an exodus, had always insisted on the church-door being left open.

But the sad story of the outrage was known too soon for the satisfaction of the faithful. A dog following a lad across a desert common had gambolled about with a bit of tinsel in his mouth, and on his master taking it from him, had returned for another piece to a suspicious-looking heap of ashes, which were all that remained of the saint.

The news of the sacrilege was bruited abroad, and two of the three actors in it were tried by the civil authorities for robbery and sacrilege; and having been executed, were hung in chains over the spot where the idol had been burnt.

Reuben Carden escaped into Holland, where he worshipped, according to the reformed religion, in such tranquillity as the remembrance of the fate of his coadjutors in the act of spoliation permitted.

The faithfulness shown by the two men, who, though tortured to reveal their accomplices, spoke no word to implicate the youth who had been in their company, mightily affected him. They died professing the reformed faith, and their constancy therein confirmed and strengthened his conviction of the truths for which they had suffered.

Silas Carden was descended from a noble family on his mother's side, who had married one of the merchant-princes of Lynn, a man of good family and great wealth. Young Silas was brought up as a courtier—'daintily from his childhood,' says the chronicle—having been tenderly and carefully nurtured, and winning man's favour by the beauty of his face and the majesty of his stature. He excelled, and was imitated and followed by, all the youth of the court. He dwelt mostly with his kinsman Lord Osford, being esteemed and beloved of all the household; and with him remained till the death of Edward the Sixth, when it seemed as though a great blight came over the land, through the reign of Mary, the persecutor of her people. Then the earl cleaving to the old faith, and Silas being a convert to that which had been stripped of its excrescences, called Protestant, departed unto his own house, where he might more freely worship God in spirit and in truth.

Now this Silas had not passed twenty-four years of life without seeking to win the love of a noble lady—the earl's daughter—who held not his creed, but that in which she had been brought up. Chrysa Vere was beloved by two suitors. She chose Silas; and the man she had rejected concealed his disappointment and rancour in becoming a professed monk in the monastery of the Gray Friars at Lynn. Thence he observed, with a heart corroded with jealousy, the happiness of the man who had been preferred to him.

Mr. Carden's absence from confession and all Catholic ceremonials soon made him a marked man; the monk of Gray Friars drawing the attention of Bishop Bonner to the fact.

When Carden's little son was born to gladden the heart of his parents, his father omitted to send for the priest to baptise him, being restrained therefrom by his dislike to the ceremonies of the Catholic Church. This disrespect was forthwith represented to Bishop Bonner by Hugo Vaughan, the monk of the Gray Friars; who gave him an order to arrest Silas, and bring him away to his palace at Fulham. It was during an evening in autumn, when Chrysa Carden sat by the large fire of piled logs, with her infant slumbering at her breast, and her head resting on the loving shoulder of her husband, whilst they murmured soft sweet talk such as young couples utter ere they have forgotten they were lovers, when looking up she perceived in the shadow of the entrance-arch the malign countenance of the man whose suit she had once wantonly encouraged, and who was now come to sate his revenge, and destroy the beautiful scene of that domestic happiness which he could never enjoy. He was followed by men-at-arms, sent by Bonner to insure obedience, should his mandate be resisted.

Chrysa started to her feet with her soul full of dread. She knew the unpitying rancour of the man whose vengeance she had provoked.

'Kiss me, Chrysa; take courage, for I bear with me the rod and staff of the Great Shepherd, even should I walk through the valley of the shadow of death; and therefore fear I no evil.'

She laid her infant in the cradle, and clung round her husband's neck in a last embrace. He whispered,

'Let me go at once, dear wife, lest the ungodly triumph in my pain.'

He departed, and the soldiers closing round him, hid him from her view. She gazed till the last of his guards had left the building; and then she turned to Hugo Vaughan, who stood in the light of the flickering flames, where her husband had a few moments before been murmuring his love-tones in her ear.

'Hugo,' she said in a hoarse hurrying voice, 'Hugo! save him—save my husband! O, Hugo! you loved me once,' she said, leaning her clasped hands on one of his arms, of which the hand was concealed within his breast. Her uplifted face was working with agony. 'You can save him if you will! O, friend! I kneel to thee, I implore thee, as my good angel!' and she clasped her arms convulsively round the knees of the monk, who looked on her with a thrill of triumph and joy.

'Canst thou plead thus for a heretic?'

'He is not a heretic; he is of the true faith,'

she cried, wild and reckless to what falsehood she gave utterance.

Hugo Vaughan said,

'It is not so, woman; and you know it is not so. You say I loved you once. Do you remember when we walked together in the old garden that you let me shred a fair tress from your young brow? It has been my companion till now; but I kept it not in love, but as an incentive to vengeance. Here it is,' drawing the tress from his bosom.

He took from the piled heap of fuel by the side of the chimney a large log, and twisting the hair around it, flung both on the blazing hearth. The sparks snapped, and flew over the floor; but the flames curled up round the goodly block, and consumed it.

'Foolish woman!' he exclaimed; 'when you trifled with me, you sowed the wind and reaped the whirlwind. As the fire circles round that burning branch of what was once a fair tree, so shall your husband Silas Carden be burned on the pile, and his ashes be scattered to the winds.'

Chrysa had clung to his knees as he continued to speak, but as he uttered the last sentence she sank on the ground insensible. He stooped and pressed his lips to hers, with a feeling of hate and love and of gratified vengeance; and then departed, leaving her lying insensible on the deer-skins which carpeted the hearth. The fire had sunk into embers, when the wail of her infant restored the unhappy woman to the consciousness of her misery.

Silas Carden was not permitted to make any preparations for his journey, and was conveyed in a carriage, lest he should attempt to escape; for his frame was large and well-knitted, and might have served to dispatch three less able men.

When he was introduced into the presence of Bonner, that cruel prelate was touched for an instant by the beauty of his countenance and the majesty of his person. He was clothed, after the fashion of the day, in a jerkin of maroon velvet, with orange-slashed sleeves, and trunk hose with slashed shoes. His hair, in short compact curls, was surmounted by a small cap of maroon velvet, ornamented with a long feather. But what surpassed all beside was, saith the chronicle, his gentle behaviour to others, and his great comeliness and stature.

'What moved you,' said the bishop, 'that ye should leave your child unchristened so long?'

'We are bound,' replied Silas, 'to do nothing contrary to the Word of God.'

'Why, baptism is therein commanded,' said the bishop.

'His institution of baptism therein I deny not,' was the answer.

'What deny ye, then?'

'I deny all things invented by man.'

'What things be there invented by man that ye be offended withal?'

'Your oil, cream, salt, spittle, candle, and conjuring of water.'

'Will ye deny what the whole world and your father hath been contented withal?

'What my father and the whole world have done I have nothing to do withal; but what God hath commanded me to do, to that stand I.'

CHAPTER XV.

'Now nearer heaven, his virtues shone more bright,
Like rising flames expanding in their height ;
The martyr's glory crown'd the soldier's fight.'

DRYDEN.

SILAS was kept in prison four months, and denied sight of his wife and infant. During this time Hugo Vaughan was ever at the side of Chrysa Carden; sometimes elating her with hope of her husband's speedy restoration to his home, at all times giving her his seeming sympathy; sometimes driving her nearly to distraction by asserting that if her husband escaped the justice of man for his heresies, the vengeance of God could not be eluded, and the fire that is not quenched would be his portion in eternity. These and suchlike discourses filled the lady's mind with profound melancholy; and setting aside as she best could the remembrance of her early teaching, she began to make diligent inquiry as to the truth of her husband's faith—a faith to which he seemed like to testify by the horror of his death as he had done by the purity of his life. A life, says the chronicle, which, in its singular love for true religion and holiness, did seem to nobilitate the cause, and shone like a pure star amidst the surrounding darkness of error.

Then she shut up her mind from the scrutiny of the monk, and pondered deeply on what course she ought to take. She was the more disposed to this course, as she had found that the monk Hugo Vaughan did but 'prophesy smooth things;' as if she had been like the children of Israel, who entreated their holy men to 'prophesy deceits.' When he visited her, he seemed to delight to raise hopes which he would dash to the ground a few weeks after, and then build up again; for he was wise in his generation, and knew that the mind will accommodate itself to the load of an inevitable grief, but not so long as hope remains that it come not.

And with the death of hope came resolution. Silas Carden was confined in Newgate; and there Chrysa, by a heavy bribe, contrived to have the following letter delivered to him:

DEAREST AND BEST OF MEN,—I will not tell thee how heavy have been my days and nights since thou wert taken from my eyes. Thy little son, who was then but three weeks old, now stands at my feet as I write; his face is wan and his movements slow, for he lives in the shadow of my great grief. O husband of my soul, I pray for thy forgiveness, if ever I grieved thee by casting doubts on the truth of thy convictions. I should have said with her of old, 'Thy people shall be my people, and thy God my God;' for my weak brain is unfitted for subtle disputations touching creeds, sacraments, masses, confessions, and prayers for the dead; and I know not if they be indeed weighty matters of the law necessary for salvation, or but the tithe of mint and anise and cummin.

My dear friend in Christ, strengthen me in the path in which I should tread; for if indeed torture and death await thee for dwelling in God's light, shall I, thy faithful wife, linger in outer darkness, and for dread of what man can do unto this frail body, choose the burning which must endure for ever and ever in hell rather than the pile of fagots which would reduce it to dust in an hour? —choose eternal separation from thee, when my soul faints that it is parted from thee for a day, and when that fiery circle of fagots shall prove but as the car of Elijah, and conduct us to heaven? I will not deny that my flesh quivers and shrinks from the torture to come. I crave for thy holy accents to whisper hope, as did the angel in the burning fiery furnace. Yet methinks I can nerve my soul by the thought that thou wilt not suffer alone. O my husband and my dear love, I know well that God's eternal truth is dearer to thee than liberty and life; that shut close in a dreary prison, there be within it solitudes and arbours of sweet meditation wherein angels may minister to thee. I have begged that he who is paid to convey this message to thee will, if possible, see thy face; that I may know from his report if thou art indeed of good comfort. I await but thy command, my husband, my guide, and my high-priest, to abstain from mass, as I have done lately from confession, and to avow my creed to be thine; that I may be in prison with thee, in bonds with thee, and, if Christ so will, in death with thee.— Thy faithful servant, CHRYSA CARDEN.

The purse of gold was heavy with which the serving-man sent by Chrysa obtained admission to Silas Carden's prison. The countenance of the prisoner yearned with strong affection when he beheld one who had just parted from his wife and

child. He never wearied with asking questions
as to how she looked; and the man replied that she
dwelt in heaviness, and faded away by slow degrees;
so that her women believed that she would not see
another spring, unless her lord should be released
out of bondage and returned to her company.

Then Silas Carden entreated the jailer to permit him to see his servant on the following morning, that he might take an answer to the writing,
which he had not yet unfolded.

A light was permitted to him by the jailer;
for men have hearts in their bosoms, and the gen-
tleness and courteous bearing of the prisoner had
softened his, all the more as he listened to the
discourse touching the wife and infant so soon to
be widowed and orphaned. How the letter written
by Chrysa pierced the heart of her husband! He
could bear the thought of the fire that should
consume his body; but at the prospect to which she
pointed, of uniting herself in his martyrdom, his
heart seemed to stand still. That fair fragile form
—could it be delivered over to the tormentors?—
clothed in serge, chained to a stake; the flames
leaping up with cruel hurry, shrivelling her soft
long hair, creeping round her fair throat, scorch-

ing her eyes, and sucking in her breath; the arms
that had so often clasped his neck tossed about
in agony and shrinking from the burning fagots;
the lips which had met his in a last kiss burnt and
bleeding!

Yet was he not bound to give her up to this
frightful death? Should he not deprive her of
salvation if he discouraged this open profession of
her faith—of faith founded on his faith? The
offer made to him by Bonner in their last interview, that he should abjure his errors, be reconciled
to the Church, and return to his home, suggested
themselves to his mind in tones of the sweetest
persuasion. Alas, he was sorely beset! He flung
himself on his knees, and rested his head on that
sacred consolation to which he ever referred his
conduct, the Bible, of which he possessed a copy
in English. He feared that in the gloom of his
cell evil spirits had power to tempt him. The Rood
of Dovercourt seemed to rise out of the shadows
and glare upon him with its ghastly eyes. Was
the trouble that had fallen upon him a judgment
for this sacrilege of his boyhood? Was he right
to set his own opinions against those of the Church
established on the rock of ages? Had he followed

a delusion, and sacrificed to it not only his worldly prosperity and his life, but hers, so far more dear to him?

As he meditated on these things, the tempter showed him as in a vision the home he had left. He seemed once more to bask in the autumn fire, with his wife clasping her infant on his breast; all the small sweet interest of home, from him so long dissevered, came back with those memories: the goodly avenue of elms that he had planted; the young fruit-trees laden with their ripening glories of gold-and-scarlet-tinted apples; the heated wall gorgeous with its velvet-coated peaches; the tawny stacks of grain in his farmyard; the noble horses that pawed the ground, and neighed when their master approached.

It was an abode of innocence and peace, of wealth distributing comfort to the needy, of innocence purifying all like a fountain of living water. He gave way to the dear delusion, dwelling on it till he slept, or rather slumbered; for he believed that he still supported his wife and child on his shoulder, in that autumn twilight by the blazing hearth, and whispered loving words and tender counsels in her ear. They spoke of the boy, whose

finger had closed round that of his father, of his
healthy form, of his future education. As his
attention was fixed on Chrysa's upturned face, he
heard a shriek. A spark had fallen on her wrap-
ping-dress; the flames darted up in spiral branches
of light, and consumed her in the arms of him,
most miserable! He saw her face of agony, he
heard her cries to him for 'Water! water!' He
started up in terror unutterable, the Bible falling
at his feet.

It awakened him thoroughly. He took up
the book with reverence.

'Thou holy volume, that dost discourse of
God's will, I implore thee to guide me in this
fearful strait.'

Then closing it sedulously, he took from his
breast a large pin, and inserted it between the
leaves, believing, with the remains of that superstition which held its thick darkness over the
ancient faith, and retained a filmy haze even over
minds more enlightened, that in the text which
first presented itself on the right hand of the
page at which the volume opened, he should find
a direction adapted for his present trouble.

This conviction was so clear in his mind, that

his pulse quickened with anxiety as he opened the book.

He read: 'Fear not them that can destroy the body, but fear Him who is able to cast both body and soul into hell.'

Silas clasped his hands and bowed his head. The voice seemed to speak his doom and that of his wife. He remained thus till dawn, and when the jailer came into the cell, he started at the change in the appearance of the prisoner.

Silas Carden wrote thus to his Chrysa:

SWEET HEART AND MOST DEAR WIFE,—That thou shouldst be brought into the way of truth and into God's presence, though the path which thither may conduct thee be dark with doubts and rough with difficulties, gives peace to my heart. Dear heart, thy messenger saith that thou art in languishing estate, and thy maidens fear for thy life. If it please God that an easier way of escape be offered to thee than by a death of torture, I should deem it one of the chiefest of His mercies. For myself, I am counted as one who goeth down into the pit.

At the last conference which that mistaken

man Bishop Bonner held with me, I declared boldly that mass was *profitless*, prayers for the dead *useless*, and calling upon or trusting in any save Jesus Christ *blasphemy;* and he answered, ' We will rid you away, and then we shall have one heretic the less.'

Yet, dear heart, the words that he also said sank deep in my memory, and did marvellously shake my resolution; for he knoweth all things of our home, doubtless from that pestilent monk Hugo Vaughan. He spoke of thee, and that thou didst pine and dwindle away with grief for my absence; and he tempted me, not as the devil did tempt Him whom I worship, with delicate meats to a starving stomach, nor with the kingdoms of the world and the glory thereof, but with that which my hungry soul doth crave more than the famished frame desireth food or the parched tongue longeth for the water-brooks—my home, my child, and thee.

My pretty one, how often, in the visions of the night, I feel the clasp of thy small hand round my finger, which was as that of a giant to thee! How often do I start, thinking I hear thy short impatient cry seeking thy mother's breast! Brief,

O, most brief, was our union on earth, beloved wife; but I count on claiming thee in the shadowless glory of heaven, where change entereth not.

I will that our little son be safely transported by safe hands to the Low Countries, where a trusty friend, Mr. Thomas Osborne, will bring him up in the fear of God, according to the tenets of the Protestant faith; for, being of tender age, I fear lest the pestilent doctrines and ceremonies of the Church of Rome should take possession of his young mind. And though he might, in the meridian of his mental and bodily strength, shake off their shackles, even as I myself have done, yet I feel by experience that there be many devils, and their name is Legion, and they lurk in ambush, and choose the seasons of mental discouragement and bodily illness to leap out upon the weakened man, and regain their influence; for they say, 'Lo, we see, and thou art blind;' and we love to trust to words that sound sweet and comforting: yet are they blind even as ourselves, and fallible, and trust to a Church built up by decrees of men, and not of Christ, the only true rule of conduct, the only infallible guide to lead to eternal life.

Be of good comfort, and know that nothing

can happen to me or to thee save by the will of God, to whose guidance and mercy I commend thee.—Thy loving husband,

SILAS CARDEN.

He was continued in prison until the February following, when he was cited to appear again in the bishop's consistory. Being there exhorted by the bishop to leave his errors and return to Mother Church, he replied,

'No, my lord, I will not; for if I had a hundred bodies, I would suffer them all to be torn in pieces rather than I will abjure or recant!'

Whereon he was condemned to be burnt on the 30th March 1555.

Now it was suggested to the bishop, that as the love borne to Silas Carden by the people of Lynn was very great, his example had seduced many from the Catholic Church who professed their convictions openly, whilst many others wavered and were inclined to heresy through the beauty of his life. Therefore this pestilent monk Hugo Vaughan did propose that the spot where he should suffer should be in the market-place at Lynn, just opposite his own house, where his servants might observe in his fate a warning to all wanderers from the true faith.

This was carried out; and on the 30th of March the pile was there erected, even as Hugo Vaughan did decree.

Chrysa Carden did, so long as she had the power, vehemently protest against the abominations of the Romish faith, and express her desire to be united to her husband both in prison and at the stake: but the first would have been a comfort not to be permitted to folks so contumacious; and for the last, God was withdrawing her with gentle hand from the world, which must be to her but full of briers and thorns for the rest of her weary pilgrimage.

When the 30th of March arrived, she was, it was said, unable to arise from her bed. In the market-place at Lynn the people closed those of their windows which looked on to the square; excepting in the house of Silas Carden, where Hugo Vaughan permitted not this indulgence to the household that considered their master's fate with such horror and pity.

The sky was heavy and loaded with vapour, and a few small flakes of snow fell. There was no wind.

'He will be longer in torture,' said Hugo Vaughan.

Now Silas Carden had given assurance to his friends and to his wife on her sick-bed as follows: a little before his death there were certain of his familiar friends and acquaintance who, being afraid by reason of the sharpness of the punishment which he was to pass through, privily desired that, even in the midst of the flames, he would show them some token, if it were possible, whereby they might be certain whether the agony of burning was so great that a man should therein keep his mind quiet and patient; which thing he promised them to do. Especially he vowed this to his poor wife, who languished on a bed of sickness from which she could never revive. It was agreed between them that if the rage and pain were tolerable and might be suffered, he should lift his hands up to heaven before he gave up the ghost.

Not long after, he was led to the place appointed for the slaughter by Lord Rich and his assistants; and being arrived at the stake, he there mildly and patiently addressed himself unto the fire, having a straight chain cast about his middle, with a multitude of people on every side compassing him about; unto whom, after he had spoken many things, especially to Lord Rich, reasoning with him on the innocent blood of the saints, after his fervent prayers made and poured out to God, the fire was set unto him. The snowflakes fell hissing on the cruel flames. It moistened the fagots, which did seem loth to consume that just man, and his torture was the greater.

There was silence in the square save the roaring of the fire—for men held their breath with awe and dread—when a scream, that seemed like the parting cry of a soul leaving its body, was heard from the house of Silas, and a wan figure leant from the open window, more like a spirit than a woman. Then, though his speech was utterly taken away by reason of the violence of the flames, his skin drawn together, the flesh of his fingers consumed by the fire, so that all men did pray that he might be unconscious of any more suffering, suddenly and contrary to all expectation, this blessed servant of God, being mindful of his promise before made, lifted up his fleshless hands in a light fire, a thing marvellous to behold, and with great rejoicing, as it seemed, struck or clapped them three times together.

At the sight of this, there arose such a shout and applause amongst the people, especially of them that understood the matter, as it might have been thought that heaven and earth were coming together. And so this blessed martyr of Christ, sinking down straightway into the fire, gave up his spirit to his Maker.*

Then there was weeping and lamentation in his household; but his wife nor wept nor made her moan, for she had departed to join him, where no tears are, nor any sorrow.

---

* The real name of Silas Carden was Thomas Haukes, a gentleman of noble descent, brought up at the court of Henry VIII., and of such comeliness of stature, such singular purity of morals, and such sweetness of disposition, that, adds the chronicle, he nobilitated the army of martyrs both by his life and by the terrible yet triumphant circumstances of his death. He suffered at Coxhall, in the manner narrated in these pages, June 10th, 1555.

CHAPTER XVI.

'He gives the winter snow her airy birth,
And bids her virgin fleeces clothe the earth.'

SANDYS.

MRS. CLEMENS heaved a heavy sigh of relief as her sister concluded the narrative.

'And the child?' gasped she at length.

'The infant was conveyed, according to his father's will, to the Low Countries, where he resided, and married a fortune and a fair wife in one. Their descendants returned here, and built this house on the site of the former one; part of the outer wall of the garden is of the original fabric, and over the door of it is a carved cornice of oak, in the centre of which are the initials S. C., intermingled with quaint devices, indicating the name of Silas Carden, or of his father.'

'Dear, dear! what an awful thing to think the poor young man was burnt over there! I wonder his people could bear to build a house just on the same spot.'

'They were justly proud of their martyred grandsire,' replied Mrs. Carden. '*I* am proud of bearing the same name.' She said this so sternly, that Nancy was silent.

When the mother and daughter went to their bedroom that night, Martha said,

'Mother, do not tell Mrs. Carden about my engagement to Philip.'

'Why, my dear?' said Mrs. Clemens, looking frightened.

'Because he is a Catholic.'

'No, my dear; I will not.'

She had already done so.

Martha peeped at her bird before she went into bed, and had the satisfaction of seeing him perched, a seeming headless tuft of downy feathers. Birds do not put their heads under their wings unless they are well and feeling happy; and Martha slept the better for that consciousness, and was awakened before it was daylight by a faint chirp, which was uttered at intervals. She had a few more crumbs on her dressing-table, which she bestowed on him, and then lay down again, glad for once that her mother's deafness prevented her being disturbed by the plaintive cry.

When the hot water was brought, and Martha arose, she looked to the window to see if it were weather in which she might safely release her prisoner; but the panes were darkened by frost, and the snow fell heavily in large flakes.

'O, dreary, dreary weather!' she cried impatiently, and her mother reminded her that it was such weather as God was pleased to send; on which Martha said in a tone which Mrs. Clemens did not hear, that it did not alter the fact of its dreariness. She had been told that there was nothing but sunshine and beautiful orange-trees where Philip was, and that was a comfort. Martha was sadly puzzled to know what was to be done with her bird when Ruth came to make the bed and dust the room. To leave it in the basket, was to subject it to the chance of having its neck wrung by the bony fingers of the hard-hearted housemaid; to move the basket to another room would attract attention. If she put the bird into a work-basket and shut down the lid, she might take it into the unused drawing-room, while her mother and aunt sat over the fire in the small sitting-room.

This she did; whilst Ruth wondered how so many bread-crumbs came to be on the dressing-table and floor. 'Queer folks to eat dry bread in their bedrooms,' she observed to her mistress.

This speech made Mrs. Carden suspicious.

When she went up to wash her hands before dinner, she went into the room occupied by her niece and sister, and found Martha happy in the delight of seeing the robin hopping about on the table with an important and self-assertive air, as if the whole world were his own. He turned his bright eye curiously on Martha, certain of her protection, and of receiving food from her hand.

'What have you here, making a mess over everything, Martha?' said her aunt's cold voice.

'A little starved robin which I picked up in the garden, nearly dead with the cold, madam,' said Martha aggressively; for she understood coming mischief in her aunt's tone.

Mrs. Carden moved to the window and threw it open; then going to the towel-horse, she took from it a towel, and began to flick the unfortunate little bird with it.

'O, aunt, don't drive him about so; you frighten him; he is so tame. You will kill him. Let me take him.' But her aunt seemed not to hear her, and succeeded in driving out the bird into the cold snowy air, and shutting the window.

Martha looked at her aunt, and if her face did not express, 'I hate you!' it told nothing of her feelings. She sat down, swelling as if her heart would burst. Mrs. Carden cared nothing for any vexation she had inflicted either on her niece or on her bird, but rang the bell for Ruth, and ordered her to bring a hand-brush and dust-pan, and to take up the crumbs. Mrs. Clemens had come into the room in the midst of the struggle; she understood Martha's face, and was filled with pity for the robin. Mr. Marchbanks had just entered the sitting-room; but of this Mrs. Carden, in her stern carrying out of the principles of cleanliness, which it was suspected she placed even higher than godliness in the list of Christian virtues, had not been aware.

Mrs. Clemens was much disturbed, and being ever ready to prodigalise sympathy, she felt a simple conviction in her own mind that she must receive it when claimed. It was this feeling which, when she was terrified by Martha's absence in the storm at Seadrift, had sent her to the house of Dr. Mereside; and it was this conviction which sent her now to Mr. Marchbanks with her little story of vexation.

'O dear, Mr. Marchbanks, I am so grieved for my poor child—that is, Martha, my daughter. She had a little tame robin that she picked up in the snow; and my sister, Mrs. Carden, she won't let it be in the bedroom because it makes untidiness, and she've turned it out all in the cold snow; and, O dear, I fear it will be froze to death, and Martha is like to break her heart. She says nothing, but I know her face. *I* can tell how bad she feels.'

Mr. Marchbanks looked quite as much concerned as Mrs. Clemens could have expected.

'Can I do anything, madam?'

'Why,' said Mrs. Clemens, fumbling in her voluminous pocket, and bringing up some silver after a lengthened search, 'if you would not mind the trouble, and would kindly take the money—a little birdcage—I should think about four-and-six-pence.'

'But the bird is gone,' suggested the merchant.

'But the weather is hard, and she may find another. My Martha is an obstinate girl when she is bent on a thing. She will break her heart if harm comes to the bird.'

'What is the young lady going to do to catch it again?'

'I don't know, I'm sure. Set the window open, I should say, as soon as my sister's back is turned.'

'I have an empty birdcage,' said the merchant. 'I will send it to you so soon as I get home.'

'O, pray don't to-night; such a dreadful night to send a poor servant out—snow so deep.'

Mr. Marchbanks had something of a smile on his face, for he had not found it so terrible. Mrs. Carden came in, and Mrs. Clemens slipped out of the room to join Martha. She found her leaning out of the window; but her aunt had taken away the candle lest it should be run down by laving in the wind, and the frightened bird could have nothing to guide him back. Mrs. Clemens' candle was not more than an inch in length, and it was soon flared down, leaving them in darkness.

'Never mind the poor little bird, Martha; you must brush your hair and put on a clean collar for dinner.'

'Do not speak to me pray, mother; I shall take no dinner unless I find the bird; and if he is killed by the cold, I will leave the house and go to service in the first place where they will take me to scrub floors, rather than live with this woman, whom I hate.'

'Hush, hush, my dear; you are angry! O, dear, to think that you call your aunt a woman! Stop! Martha, where are you going?'

'Into the garden to try to find it,' replied the daughter with an elevation of voice intended to reach her mother, who was deaf and stood at the top of the stairs, when she had reached the landing.

Martha was too angry to care if all the world heard her. Mr. Marchbanks had just left the sitting-room.

'Pardon me, ma'am,' he said, laying his hand gently on her arm; 'your going in the dark is pretty well useless. Take this lantern,' continued he, placing a neat brass lantern in her hand, with which he was accustomed to thread the streets of Lynn, not then too well lighted.

Martha was grateful for the aid, and without stopping to care or to inquire how he could understand her intention, she walked out underneath the cedar-trees and then stood still, whistling in a low tone. The flakes of snow fell fast on her bosom, and the keen wind rushed by her, but the tiny bird gave no response to her voice.

'That woman no doubt hurt him with the towel; probably he has fallen down just outside the window, too bruised to fly.'

She acted on the thought, and searched the ground below the window. There was a deep space, to admit of light been thrown into the underground kitchen, of which the window-shutters were closed. Martha thought she perceived a little dark lump on the snow, and turning off it the light of the lantern she saw, O joy! her robin, though looking very forlorn, with his feet cramped by the cold, and the film drawn over his eyes. She took him up very tenderly and placed him in her bosom.

'I wonder if he is hurt, if he will recover. Where shall I go with him—what can I do? I must give this lantern back to the gentleman;' and with one hand pressed to her breast where the robin was laid, and the lantern in the other, she returned to the house. .

'You have got him again,' said Mr. Marchbanks.

'Yes, thank you very much. I could not have found him but for your lantern.'

'You require a cage. I will send one up at once. 'Tis no trouble,—no expense; mine is empty.'

'O dear, how very kind of you!' said Martha, really touched and grateful; 'but I fear my aunt will not let me keep it. I only want it to stay till the weather is warmer, poor little bird!'

And as she leant her head tenderly towards

the side of her bosom where the bird was laid, Mr. Marchbanks thought how feminine and charming she looked.

He knew the characters with whom she had to deal, and thought it not unlikely that Ruth or Mrs. Carden would dismiss the bird, though it were rendered by the cage comparatively harmless. Birds in cages, however, are apt to disperse the shells of their seeds in unsightly circles on the carpet; sometimes they attempt the luxury of a bath, and send sprinklings of water in the same direction.

'If you can contrive to keep your bird till I bring a cage, I think I can relieve you of some of your perplexities,' Mr. Marchbanks said. 'It is not far; I will be back again in ten minutes;' and he disappeared.

Martha held the bird on her breast, and stood outside the door leading to the garden. Here Ruth found her, with the information that dinner was ready.

'Tell your mistress that I do not take any,' Martha replied curtly.

Ruth delivered the message, adding, if possible, bitterness to its tone.

Mrs. Clemens rose from the dinner-table, at

which she was seated with her sister, with much disturbance, to seek her daughter.

'Sit still, Nancy,' her sister said, with a commanding accent. 'If Martha is out of temper, she is better out of the room than in it. I am not going to allow my house to be made a pig-sty to please her, or any one else.'

'No, sister, of course not; only one little bird could not do much harm, and'—and here Nancy began to cry—'I can't eat a morsel if I think my girl is hungry.'

'Leave it, then. I take it you will both find your appetites, bird or no bird, before to-morrow morning.' And Mrs. Carden ate her dinner, not without some irritation at the sobs and sniffs to which her sister gave utterance behind her pocket-handkerchief.

'Why should *I*, the mistress of this house,' thus ran her meditations, 'having escaped the infliction of the dirt and untidiness of children, and taking a pleasure in perfect neatness for nearly thirty years, now put up with the upsetting of all my notions and habits, for the sake of a sulky young woman, who, never having had costly furniture about her, does not care how she destroys mine?'

For Ruth had shown her the desecrated basket, led to its inspection by the projecting end of the temporary perch, and had pointed out below the corner where the robin had reposed certain indications that the basket must be relined. To be sure the pink calico had faded to a dirty yellow; but it would have lasted *her* life without the necessity of renewal; and she felt herself injured to the amount of five shillings and ninepence in her pocket, and much more in the insult to her authority.

CHAPTER XVII.

'House-room, which costs him nothing, he bestows.'
                                        DRYDEN.

THE ten minutes seemed lengthened into twenty before Martha heard the ring at the front door which announced the return of Mr. Marchbanks. Martha hastened to open it herself, for Ruth was in the dining-room, waiting at dinner.

There he stood, with his lantern in one hand, and a cage and a large key in the other.

'Will you intrust me with the bird?'

Martha shook her head.

'Men are generally such brutes,' she said bluntly.

He smiled.

'Women also,' he replied, 'sometimes. But there is an empty house at a short distance from hence, of which I am the landlord. I thought you might like me to put the bird into one of the rooms in the open cage, and it could fly about without interference from any one.'

'How very good! how very thoughtful!' said Martha. 'But I should like to place it there myself.'

He looked at her shoes, and said doubtfully,

'The snow is very deep.'

'I do not regard weather,' replied Martha. 'If you please, I had rather go and see it myself.'

'Come, then,' he said. 'Will you accept my arm?'

Martha declined; but before she had proceeded five steps she slid, and nearly fell. He offered his arm silently a second time, and Martha, glad of the support, did not again refuse to avail herself of it.

In a few minutes they reached the stone flight of steps, and Mr. Marchbanks kicked away some of the snow from the front door before he opened it. The hall looked dark and uninviting.

'Yes, it is dreary,' he said, answering what he believed to be Martha's feeling; 'but the walls are very solid, and the rooms will be less cold than the night atmosphere in the garden.'

He opened the door of a lofty room, and placed the cage on a marble slab.

'There is seed in the trough,' he said; 'and if you will remain here in the darkness for a moment, I will procure him some water.'

He vanished with the lantern, leaving Martha standing in the gloom of such light as was reflected on the marble wall from the snow outside. She still held the bird on her breast, and waited first five minutes, then ten, then twenty, till she was oppressed by a nameless terror. All was so still. She knew not which way Mr. Marchbanks had disappeared. She was by no means an imaginative person, yet she began to conjure up all sorts of accidents as the cause of his not returning. Suppose he should have gone to draw water from a well, and have fallen in. Suppose he had come upon some concealed burglars, who had dispatched him for discovering them. Martha might have made a brave man, for the thought of danger always nerved her to meet it.

'There are all kinds of dreary hiding-places in

this house, seemingly,' she said. 'He probably went downstairs as it was to fetch water;' and she felt with one hand and both feet to the top of what she supposed to be the kitchen-stairs. 'Mr. Marchbanks! Mr. Marchbanks!' she cried, the last time rather tremulously.

She stopped to listen, and fancied she heard a remote footstep. Presently a light shone from a distant passage, and Mr. Marchbanks appeared.

'I am so ashamed of keeping you so long in the dark, Miss Clemens; but I have been trying to light the fire,—otherwise there will be no water for the bird, all the taps being frozen.'

'Dear me! would not a little snow do?—it might melt, you know.'

'I fear it would be more likely to freeze. The fire is beginning to burn, and the taps will soon feel its influence. I found some coals and a few sticks left here by the last tenant.'

'The bird will not want water to-night,' said Martha; 'but I am very grateful to you all the same. As the fire is burning, perhaps it would be better to leave the cage here to feel the benefit of the warmth.'

'I will go up and fetch it,' said the merchant, who, though he was

' An honest man, close button'd to the chin,
  Broadcloth without and a warm heart within,'

felt his teeth chattering with cold, and longed to
go back to his own fire, after trying to kindle this
alien one.

'Please come back soon,' said Martha, fearing
she might wander about in the underground pass-
ages all night, if he did not return with the light.

This time, however, he did not keep her waiting. The cage was deposited on a dresser opposite
the fire, though at some distance. The bird being
placed inside, it fluttered an instant, and then remained with outstretched wings against the wires.

'Poor darling! he is so frightened,' she said
apologetically. 'He will get better in a few minutes.'

She went, following Mr. Marchbanks to the
kitchen-door, filled with pity and apprehension at
the thought of the robin's being the only living
thing in that dark dreary house, and she was
going away from him. She returned, and hung
her shawl over the cage, and returned again, after
reaching the kitchen-door.

'I am afraid,' said she timidly (for her), 'that
you think me very foolish; but suppose that a rat
or a cat should find my bird. If you did not mind

lifting the cage, and hanging it on that nail, I should be so thankful.'

Mr. Marchbanks obeyed, and arranged the shawl over the cage.

'Anything else ?' he said.

'No, thank you.'

'Then we will go ;' and he lighted Martha up the kitchen-stairs, through the hall, and out of the door, which he locked.

Then they walked in silence back to the house of Mrs. Carden, where, when arrived, the merchant gave Martha the key, and bowing, left her.

The merchant had been torn by his feelings of compassion and his notions of propriety as they trod over the snow in the silent square. He knew the wind blew keenly on the uncovered shoulders of Martha, denuded of her shawl; but his buttoned-up coat did not cover an undercoat; and though he would have borne the cold willingly to shield the woman at his side, the idea that any one should meet him walking with a female in his shirt-sleeves at that time of night would be a dreadful imputation on his character, even if he could bring himself to commit an act of such impropriety as to strip himself of his upper garment in her presence. As it was, he walked home, thinking what he ought to have done, and speculating whether Miss Clemens would catch inflammation of the lungs and die; and comforting himself by the reflection that he had been very good-natured altogether, and could not have been expected to give himself a chance of cold, to save her from the infliction.

Then conscience made herself unpleasant by the suggestion that *his* shoulders, under the stout Irish shirt, were comforted by a warm flannel waistcoat, made for him by that dear saint in heaven, his deceased wife; whilst Martha's skin looked pink and white under what ladies called a muslin habit-shirt; for Martha had just dressed for her aunt's dinner in the best way she could, to please that particular lady, when the fracas occurred.

Then he thought how fond Mary had been of him, and how vexed she would have been had he run the risk of taking cold for a stranger; and he was comforted, and thought he had been quite right after all. She had pleased herself by wrapping the bird-cage with her shawl, and there was no reason why he should suffer for her humanity.

When Martha tried the door, it gave way to her pressure; for in her anxiety to go out silently, not to alarm her mother, she had not turned the handle, and consequently it had not caught the lock. She felt her way up to her room, smoothed her hair, and came down to the sitting-room with a quiet expression of face, which arose from a feeling of satisfaction at having succeeded in making the bird comfortable, but in which Mrs. Carden read submission, and her anxious mother depression. Martha did not see the loving eyes turned on her so inquiringly. Mrs. Clemens had only been prevented going to her bedroom to look for Martha by Mrs. Carden's reproaches and assurances that her sister knew nothing of the management of children (an assertion frequently enunciated by persons who have not borne any), and that if she sat still, Martha would come down presently, very cold and very repentant. Mrs. Clemens did not doubt the first, but was sceptical as to the repentance. She knew Martha, with the bitter experience of twenty-seven years.

Though Martha had but a slow perception of humour, she could not help what Leigh Hunt calls an 'inward smile,' when she thought how overwhelming would be the rage of her aunt if she could know that the manager—her own property, as she seemed to consider him—had aided and abetted her niece in her rebellion to her auntly authority.

Mrs. Carden sat more upright than ever, casting satisfied glances on Martha, whom she had brought, as she believed, into a properly repentant frame of mind. She speculated whether her niece would not say how sorry she was that she had vexed her aunt presently. As Martha did not speak, but looked very placid, Mrs. Carden thought she had better suggest it. Then she reflected that if Martha rebelled, it would be very unpleasant, as she was too old to be whipped or locked up without her food; so she let well alone, and went on with her knitting. Poor Mrs. Clemens tried hers; but she had wept so much, that her eyes were watery and dim, and her hands shook too much to guide the needles. Each of the party was pleased when the clock chimed half-past nine, when prayers were read by Mrs. Carden; and the mother and daughter retired to their sleeping-room.

'O, Martha dear,' said Mrs. Clemens, 'where is the poor little bird? I am afraid as of my life that sister will find him; for I knew when you came in that he was safe, or you would not have come.'

'He *is* safe, mother. Be satisfied.'

'But *where*, my dear? If you have him in the

chest of drawers or the wardrobe, they will find him, and turn him out again.'

'He is safe, mother; and I want to go to sleep,' replied Martha, who distrusted her mother's powers of reticence.

When she awoke in the gray dawn of continued frost, she got up quietly, and taking the large key, went out of the front door, away to the empty house. The warmth of the embers in the large kitchen-grate still lingered; and Martha, finding some sparks yet left, rekindled the fire, thinking she might take that liberty with the unclaimed coals. First she uncovered the robin; and was glad to find him busy in his toilet, pluming himself and arranging the feathers, which the violent attack of the towel had displaced, and which his confinement on Martha's bosom had not tended to replace. She drew some water from the thawed tap for his fountain; and having placed him where there was most light, left him, lest her surreptitious visit should be traced.

The next time Mr. Marchbanks came, he bowed to Miss Clemens with a peculiar look of intelligence, which the elder matrons did not perceive. His glance said, 'How is the bird? and I don't think you look as if you had caught cold, as I fully believed you would have done.' Something of this he expressed in a general way:

'I hope you ladies have not suffered from this bitter east wind. I imagine not, judging from your appearance.' And he bowed to the three with a clean sweep, but with an unmistakable look at Martha.

Mrs. Carden replied that, always inhaling a moderately warmed atmosphere, she thought there was little danger of suffering from any change of the weather outside. When they went out, she said, it was in a close carriage.

He smiled and bowed again; and on being detained with regard to some last instructions as to the business letters, he remained a few minutes longer; so that Martha, who had gone upstairs to fetch a ball of knitting-cotton for her mother, encountered him on her descent as he was leaving the hall.

'I hope he is well,' Mr. Marchbanks said.

'Quite, thank you,' replied Martha, blushing, she scarcely knew why.

'I have been sadly uneasy lest you should have taken cold,' said the merchant. 'I thought I ought not to have allowed you to sacrifice your health for the bird.'

'O, you are very kind,' replied the girl, blushing still deeper.

Ruth came bustling up to open the door for the manager, who went away thinking how very lovely Miss Clemens was when she blushed. He supposed she was very shy; or why should she change colour? Then he thought, with a creeping sensation of cold down his back, of that rigid outstretched form which awaited him in his house. I believe men never long so much for the companionship of a second wife as in the sudden horrors of their loss of the first.

When Mrs. Carden, tired by the perseverance of the frost, had had her horses roughed, and had gone out with Mrs. Clemens, Martha took her key fearlessly, and went off to the empty house. It was lucky for the comfort of the robin that the frost broke up before the supply of coal was exhausted.

One morning, when the garden glittered in the new-born sunbeams of March, and even the massive cedars looked as if inspired by fresh life in their fibrous foliage—when there was no longer dread lest he should feel the heart-gnawing pangs of hunger, nor the stupefying pain of cold—Martha placed the bird on the window-sill of the empty house.

He looked at her askance for a moment with his merry bright eye, and then spreading his reckless wings, he flew away to enjoy liberty. Martha left the window open, and some food in his cage. He did not return, as she had half hoped he would.

Time went on steadily in the oak mansion at Lynn, with little perceptible variation. Mrs. Clemens felt the influence of better food and the absence of anxiety as to how it was to be obtained. Her pretty old fair face plumped up—it was too delicate even to look coarse—and her appearance was improved by some handsome gowns given her by Mrs. Carden, who felt a reflected pride in having her sister well dressed. The reed which bends to the blast has a better time of it than the rock which is a resisting body. There was a spirit of rebellion in Martha which made her antagonistic to her aunt. No prospect of inheriting her wealth, the disposition of which after her death must so greatly affect Martha's future life, could produce in this young woman the slightest subservience. Her heart was not like that of her mother—a well of tenderness bubbling over on every creature within her reach. Mrs. Clemens would have divided her last crust with her bitterest enemy, if she ever could have had one, and given him the largest share, concealing from him that she had done so, if possible, to save his feelings. Martha would pay back injury by injury to the uttermost. Her perceptions were dull, and her affections slow to take root; but once established, they could never be shaken. The logs of wood which burn longest and fiercest are not those which kindle most easily. She was mostly tranquil, however; for she was not acute at perceiving slights or offences, and her aunt did not ever offer any when her ideas of propriety as to tidiness and cleanliness were not opposed. Martha learnt to keep a pair of slippers downstairs, where she might take off her walking-shoes before she trod on the handsome carpets. She was always disposed to silence, so did not offend her aunt by talking. She felt, as did her mother, the change for the better in the food, and grew five years younger in appearance in the first twelve months of their residence with Mrs. Carden. Her fingers became rounded, and lost the ugly marks of the needle. Mrs. Carden was liberal in giving her clothes—less handsome than those she bestowed on Nancy, but better than Martha had ever allowed herself to purchase since she had been bread-winner for her mother and herself. The other person of the trio showed no outward improvement; on the contrary, the lines deepened on her face; the features became more pointed, and her tint was sometimes gray, sometimes flushed with fever. She walked with more deliberation, and was careful not to jolt herself by any sudden movement. Sometimes she was evidently in pain, and under these circumstances she did not speak till the spasm had passed away.

'O Betsy, I'm sure you are suffering agony!' said Mrs. Clemens one day, when she looked up on receiving no answer, and observed the corrugations on her sister's brow.

'What if I do suffer?' she replied, when she could speak. 'It cannot be so bad as being burnt to death like Silas Carden.'

Martha had made an opportunity, blushing again as she did so at the clandestine nature of the communication, to tell Mr. Marchbanks that she was very much obliged for the use of the cage, and that he would find it in his house, of which she remitted to him the key. He was glad to have been of use to her, he said; and there ended the matter, so far as Martha was concerned. Mr. Marchbanks too became accustomed to the loneliness of his home, and was less anxious for a companion in his solitude. Of course he, who dwelt in decencies for ever, could not think of another Mrs. Marchbanks for twelve months; and then—why, then he thought that Martha was a very nice-looking girl, and that she would probably inherit the wealth which he and Mrs. Carden were so eager to accumulate.

Two years passed without much alteration in the circumstances of two of the trio in the old oak mansion in the market-place of Lynn; but each month withdrew strength from, and increased suffering to, the mistress of the house. Now she no longer ventured to move about, for the result of doing so might be immediate death. She was dressed in a wrapping-gown, and lay on the sofa all day. Mr. Marchbanks, as usual, brought letters and received instructions, and sent inquiring glances to the door when he heard the handle turn, hoping that Martha might open it, and generally was disappointed.

One day, after a night of exhausting pain had made Mrs. Carden weaker than usual, she spoke seriously to her sister.

'Nancy, I've had as much as I can manage to bear pretty well. I don't wish to die, but I see no chance of life holding out under such agony;

so I am going to make my will. I may have
been too fond of money; and people who have a
good deal, and have made a good deal, ought to
be careful that it don't do harm after they are
dead, instead of good. You know, Nancy, you
are older than I am, and to leave it all to you
would be folly; so, my dear, tell me how many
hundreds a year you want for your comfort—and
don't be *skimpy*—and I will give you a charge on
the estate for your life.'

'Bless me, sister, for myself? Why, a hundred a year would be plenty!'

'You always were a fool, Nancy; but you'll
muddle away the money if you have it, very likely,
or give it where I don't choose it should go.
However, I'll make it 300*l.* a year, and that will
keep you above want for your life. Now as to
Martha—'

There was a pause, and Mrs. Clemens looked
anxiously at the sick woman; for she feared something unpleasant was at hand. Mrs. Carden raised
herself on her elbow, and peered out on the market-place, which was now empty, as it was not
market-day.

'Do you see where that lamp-post stands?'

'Yes, sister.'

'I had it put there. There is an inscription on the stone that supports the iron of the lamp—"A lantern to my feet, and a light to my path." It means that on that spot Silas Carden made a warning light to all, what to follow and what to shun.'

'Yes, sister,' gasped out poor Mrs. Clemens.

'Now, Nancy, attend to what I am going to say. Not one penny of mine shall ever go to a Catholic, nor to any one who marries a Catholic. Why, 'twould be enough to bring together again all the scattered ashes of that blessed saint's tortured body to reproach me, if I did such a thing! I will not do it, Nancy. The money accumulated by the descendants of Silas Carden shall not go to build up another circle of fagots and burning tar, to burn those who cleave to the truth.'

'But, sister,' said Mrs. Clemens, 'folks don't burn people now.'

'And why don't they? Because the Protestants have the upper hand; if the Catholics were once in their ancient sway, they would light as many fires as did that compound of lust and bigotry who thought to win caresses from a loathing husband by making continual burnt-offerings to him of human flesh and blood.'

'But, sister,' reiterated Mrs. Clemens, 'folks don't burn people now—'tis against the law.'

'And who makes the law, I wonder, you noodle-headed old woman?'

'Why, them that's in power, to be sure.'

'Well, and if those bloody-minded Catholics were in power again, would not they burn us?'

'God forbid!' murmured Nancy. 'I don't think Philip would ever have the heart to burn Martha or me. Besides, they have no power now,' reiterated the poor old woman, coming back to the safest ground.

'I tell you what, Nancy—' then breaking off suddenly, 'Why did they burn Silas Carden?'

'I suppose the poor ignorant misguided folks knew no better,' suggested Mrs. Clemens.

'Exactly so. But who misguided them?'

'Them as was over them,' said the elder sister, detecting a tone of triumph in the invalid, which was as prescient of victory as the shout with which Napier declares the British soldier inaugurates his attack on the enemy.

. 'Them as was over them were *Catholics*,' said Mrs. Carden, repeating her sister's bad grammar. 'The people were misguided because guided by *them*. They were thus guided because they were ignorant. 'Tis only by keeping men ignorant they can be thus led; and the Catholic religion is one which tends to slavery and ignorance, because they are afraid that people should read and judge for themselves. When I leave my will about my husband's money, would you believe what people said about it, without reading it for yourself? What would you think of anybody who said, " You are interested in knowing the contents of this will, but we are going to lock it up that you may not read it" ?'

' Well, that would seem hard,' said Nancy.

' And,' said Mrs. Carden, ' that's what the Catholics do with the Bible, which is the will of God.'

' But, Betsy, suppose you had a son who was wicked, would you keep him out always, and say, " You shall not come in and fare with the rest, because you were wicked once" ? I think, after he had suffered a good while, I would say, " Come in now; for you have been punished a long time." So the Catholics should be forgiven.'

' So,' said the invalid in great wrath, ' you have been sucking in these Catholic heresies of purgatory? I'm ashamed of you, Nancy! Well, I thank God,' she continued, ' the money is in my

own hands *yet;* and I am a good Church-woman
enough to die happy in the belief that the Catholics who burned people for telling the truth will
burn for ever and ever in hell-fire for teaching lies.'

' O, Betsy !'

'Yes; 'tis a comfort for a true Christian in
dying to believe in the eternity of hell torment.
Now especially 'tis everybody's duty to set themselves against innovation; for—will you believe
it ?—they are trying and trying to bring these
pestilent heretics into power again. Catholic
emancipation they call it. 'Tis as if the father
of a family had destroyed all the wolves in his
neighbourhood, seeing a fresh litter, and having
forgotten that they rent and destroyed his ancestors, he says, " Poor darlings ! pretty gentle
things ! Let them come in and warm themselves."
But where's the use of talking to you, who have no
sense ? Tell me a few facts: you said Martha is
engaged to this young Jack Spaniard?'

' His name is not Jack, but Philip, sister.'

'Well,' angrily, ' what matters it?'

. ' Yes ; she is engaged to him.'

' Do they correspond ?'

'Bless you, no. He does not know how to
write English.'

'A fine fool he must be ! And you have lived here two years and heard nothing from him ?'

' No.'

' No message sent over by word of mouth ?'

' No.'

' Well, Nancy, Martha may do as she pleases; but the young man may be dead, or, if alive, he has certainly forgotten her. She's a fool if she waits for him; moreover, if my eyes don't deceive me, Mr. Marchbanks thinks Martha would make him a good wife; I know he would make her a good husband. Then the money would all be kept together, and be properly spent — not thrown away on drones in convents, who think they make a claim on heaven by making other people work for them on earth. I will thank you,' continued Mrs. Carden, 'sister, to call Martha up; and let me have her answer—yes or no —whether she means to marry that young Papist or not.'

Mrs. Clemens felt her heart sink down into her shoes. How could she confess to Martha that she had mentioned her engagement to her aunt, in the very teeth of her request that she should not do so ? The timid and irresolute always cling to postponement.

'Martha has stepped out, Betsy. It will do when she comes back, won't it?'

'Umph! Yes; but it must be settled to-day.'

Mrs. Clemens felt sick with apprehension. Something must be said or done. This timid woman was afraid of her daughter and afraid of her sister. In the first exuberance of confidence, and full of the pleasure and importance of having something about her daughter's attractions to communicate, she had told her sister the story of Philip's engagement to Martha, and had repented it ever since: first, when she had seen Betsy's face cloud over during her recital, when she had then gone too far to stop; secondly, when Martha had given her warning, too late for anything but repentance: and lastly, now, when she knew not how to break the truth to her daughter, that her advice had come when it was useless. About what course was to be adopted, she knew nothing. She was so drifted about, frail bark that she was, by different feelings and veering opinions, that she resigned herself to do what those whom she loved desired most.

She had been very fond of Philip; but then, as she said, they had seen 'neither feather nor bone of him' for two years; and he might be dead.

And here was Mr. Marchbanks—such a handsome, kind, wealthy man—would make Martha an excellent husband; and it certainly would be nicer to have grandchildren who went to church or chapel like Christians, rather than to have a set of young Papists, worshipping little dolls, and calling them holy Jesuses.

And then, they would be rolling in riches: Mrs. Carden would leave them all her wealth; and not a penny to Martha if she married Philip.

How could she marry Philip? He was not there to be married. How could they know he would even come back? Really Martha would prove herself a very foolish wilful girl if she did not do what her aunt wished on this occasion. She would send Ruth to sit by her mistress, and go out to look for Martha, and reason with her on the subject.

CHAPTER XVIII.

' Your beauty that did haunt me in my sleep.'
SHAKESPEARE.

WHEN Martha had given her robin his liberty
in the strange garden, she had had a natural wish
to see him again. The same architect had designed
both houses—that in which Mrs. Carden resided
and the one belonging to Mr. Marchbanks—which
had belonged originally to two brothers. The
same gardener had designed the garden of each
house. Smaller dwellings intervened with their
more diminutive plots of ground; but the ladies
of the two mansions had caused to be enclosed an
avenue of elms at the extremity of their gardens,
which avenue ran parallel with the houses, making in conjunction with the gardens three sides of
a square.

Mr. Marchbanks had given Martha a key to
this avenue and to the grounds of the deserted
house, that she might carry on her interviews with
her robin. She was fond of escaping from her
aunt and mother, and walking or sitting alone
under the cedar-trees, which had circular seats
round them, not yet rotted away entirely by the

weather. She knew no one in Lynn, and cared not to go out into strange places now that she had walked over the town once. Her mother, trusting her word that she would not go beyond the garden, was not nervous when she disappeared for a couple of hours, as she used frequently to do with her sewing or knitting—but not with a book, for Martha was no reader. She thought of the man she loved so tenderly with a heart-sick longing to see or hear something from him. She had the firmest faith in his returning to her. He had said it; he would accomplish it under all difficulties.

She lingered longer than usual on this day in her loitering walk to the garden of the empty house; and having reached it, she sat down in a little sequestered nook, formed by an angle of the wall and a half-uprooted yew-tree, whose branches swept the ground, and would have concealed her from observation, had there been any to observe.

It was a bright day, late in autumn, and the sun shot its slant rays over the ruined garden, and the careless beauties of vegetation, which with lavish growth strove to conceal the dilapidation of time. There was the greenhouse, with the broken panes of glass, out of which wandered the tendrils of unpruned vines. One large branch had chosen to spring from the root outside, and had supported itself on the funnel of a stove which projected from the wall, round which it flung its graceful tendrils and its brown - red branches, laden with diminutive grapes in compact clusters, shaded by crimson and yellow leaves. Some gourd plants trailed their golden fruit over the weed-covered ground, and abundance of apples lay in ungathered heaps. At the end of the greenhouse there was a small low building, which had contained the fireplace. Some of the tiles stood in their places—smooth and red once, but now covered with rough patches of bright yellow, gray, pink, blue, and white lichen. Through the open spaces in the roof the vine found its way, and hung its purple berries over the old oak door, which rested on one hinge. It was so long since it had been moved, that the clusters had bloomed, formed their berries, and swelled into size and colour. One bunch, half divided by the edge of the door, must have been crushed had it been moved an inch either way. There was a heavy stone roller, nearly covered by the weeds that had crept over it. These fell in tendrils and creepers

of unusual grace from the circular form to which
they clung, and from which they depended. A
long avenue of cedars led up to the house, and
Martha's nook commanded a view of its extent.

As Martha looked at all I have described, but
saw nothing—for she had small perception of picturesque beauty—she heard a voice singing, which
made her hold her breath to listen, so powerful,
rich, and sweet were its tones ; and a moment after
it sang,

> ' As he comes marching up the street
> The pipes sound shrill and clear.'

The songstress appeared through the open door
of the house, coming down the fibre-covered path,
on which the cedars had spread their accumulated
deposit of years, and singing to herself as the birds
sing—from the pleasure of existence.

How beautiful this young creature was ! She
was dressed in a light-blue muslin, drawn up in the
fashion called *à la vierge,* allowing the throat to
be seen, and a small portion of the neck in a circle
below it. Her hair, which was of a golden brown,
fell in curls round her head. She held a hat in
her hand, and was looking round her with an air
of curiosity and interest.

Martha knew the creature who stood there in

the sunshine; she knew her from her old enmity towards the petted child at school, and from the jealousy which she had felt when Philip copied her portrait.

'O, she is too, too lovely,' cried poor Martha to herself. 'Such creatures ought not to live, to make common folks wretched.'

'Charlie is my darling, my darling, my darling!' the girl continued to sing, throwing a tone of intense tenderness into the high notes of 'The Young Chevalier.'

As she gazed and sang, a lady joined her from the house. She was taller and larger built than the younger lady—in deep mourning, in a widow's bonnet, from which a large crape veil descended, which, being thrown back, revealed a fair skin, a large red mouth, small eyes set closely together, and a quantity of light hair falling each side of her face in ringlets. The dull unglossy material of the dress, deeply trimmed with crape, which was even less reflective of the sunshine than the dress itself, threw into brilliant contrast the figure of the young girl, as the elder lady stood by her side, and looked around her, as did her companion. But her countenance became more speculative than pleased at the prospect.

'What a scene of desolation!' said she.

'*How* can you say so! I never saw anything so beautiful, so picturesque!'

'Think what it will cost to put into order,' said the widow.

'Must it be put into order?'

'My dear, fancy a garden in this state!'

Martha lost the next few words; and then the girl said,

'— would make such beautiful studies of it as it is.'

Martha could not catch the name. It sounded like Rosa, she thought. Could Rosa be Philip? Martha would not believe it. Rosa was some girl-friend. There was a Rosa, of whom the child used to speak when she was at school—her stepsister. It must have been this girl to whom she referred.

The strangers returned to the house; and Martha retired silently through the garden-door, locking it after her, where she would have liked to shut up the ladies in it for ever.

————

CHAPTER XIX.

'A woman yet must blush, when bashful is the case.'

THE delay which Mrs. Clemens had so desired occurred. Mrs. Carden, exhausted by a restless night and excessive pain, and by the irritation of finding her favourite ideas not responded to by her sister, had fallen asleep when Martha reached the house. Mrs. Clemens was grateful for the delay, and lost courage to speak to Martha about the secret she had revealed.

When Mrs. Carden awoke, it was from hearing the peculiar ring and knock which announced the manager — an indication to which she had been accustomed to watch for so many years.

Mrs. Clemens and Martha sat in the window in the autumn twilight; Mr. Marchbanks by the side of the sofa, with a single candle on the little table, by which he read his business letters.

'I think,' he said, when he had concluded his task and received his instructions, 'that I may have the good luck to let that house of mine at last. A widow lady, who has to retire from the mansion to which her husband's heir has brought his bride, seems inclined to take it if we can agree about the rent. She asked me if it were furnished; but I said it contained only an empty birdcage.'

As Mr. Marchbanks spoke thus his eyes sought a recognition in those of Martha. She had looked up with interest when he talked of letting the house, and he met her glance before she dropped her eyelids again. He had long been trying in small ways to recommend himself to her. As her mother always seemed uneasy when she walked out in the town, Mr. Marchbanks often volunteered to purchase cotton for knitting or lamb's-wool for embroidery. Sometimes he brought a bunch of grapes or a melon, which he fancied Martha would like the dignity of possessing even if she cared not for the fruit; and satisfied by her mute and blushing acceptance of these offerings, he ventured at length to send to the oak mansion a box containing a chinchilla muff and tippet, addressed to Miss Clemens.

Martha was sitting by her aunt's couch when the parcels arrived, and flushed to a deep pink when she opened them.

'O, I can't indeed!' she said, looking at them in dismay.

'Can't what?' cried her aunt sharply.

'Can't accept anything which cost him so much money.'

'Bless you, he did not purchase these for *you!* They belonged to his wife. She only received them the day before she was taken ill. As Mr. Marchbanks can't go about in a muff and tippet, however cold it may be, and as the moths will probably devour the skins if he keeps them any longer, he could not do better than give them to you or your mother. Your mother always has my sables now that I can't go out; so he has given them to you, because you had none. Write a note and say you are much obliged.'

Martha was a poor scribe.

'I will thank him when he comes,' said Martha, after having sat uncomfortably during all the interview, feeling too shy to express her gratitude before her mother and aunt, but thinking that it *must* be done; turning over in her mind all the difficulties of penmanship with a conviction, that she should make some mistake before she had covered half a page of note-paper if she tried to write what ought to be said, yet, now that the difficulty of speaking was present, and the materials of penmanship absent, that the latter was the easiest.

She rose suddenly when Mr. Marchbanks left the room, and followed him down to the door. He had his hand on the handle, when he heard the rustle of her dress behind him, and felt his heart beat fast. Hearts beat quite as hurriedly, young folks, after forty-four as at twenty-four.

The door-lamp shone on Martha's rippled hair and on her face, which was flushed and tremulous with an emotion born of nervousness. There was something which seemed to her uncanny in the thought of wearing his dead wife's furs; yet she wanted them very much, and her aunt had desired her to accept them.

'Mr. Marchbanks,' she began, holding out her hand for a parting good-night, 'I cannot tell you how grateful I am for your very costly gift — so costly, that I hesitate to accept it.'

'You will confer a favour on me by wearing the furs, Miss Clemens. I shall wish to offer you another gift one day. I hope you will receive that as condescendingly as you will make me happy by accepting this.'

He pressed her hand tenderly, and went out.

'I ought to have spoken then,' he thought; 'but it was so awkward, standing on the doormat, and the chance of Ruth coming up every minute.'

Of two shy people, the woman, as usual, had expressed herself most gracefully; but she had the advantage of conning her little speech all the way downstairs, and Mr. Marchbanks, not expecting her, was unprepared with an answer.

Martha went upstairs again, feeling that she had done her duty, and might enjoy the thought of her furs in peace. She had not given much attention to the manager's allusion to the future gift. Her aunt had told her to accept the chinchilla furs, but she did not feel comfortable in the thought of wearing the dead wife's gear. It was all nonsense, of course; but still there was something gruesome in the notion.

CHAPTER XX.

'If men would not exhale vapours to cloud and darken the clearest truths, no man could miss his way to heaven for want of light.'   BROWNE.

'And ever and anon a doleful knell
Comes from the fatal owl, that in sad mood
With dreary sound doth pierce through the death-shadow'd
wood.'
                                      MORE'S *Song of the Soul.*

MRS. CARDEN had to sit up with her as nurse either her sister or Martha half of each night, and Ruth the other half alternately with a hired nurse, knowing that the comfort of a patient depends on the alertness of the watcher, and on her sweetness of temper, a quality difficult to retain when the brain is irritated by wakefulness.

It was Martha's turn that night to begin her watch at eleven o'clock, when the patient was shut up for the night, and to remain till half-past three, when Mrs. Clemens got up and took her place.

Night seems to bring a mysterious and malign influence on those who are either bodily or mentally ill at ease. To Mrs. Carden it brought fever and increased pain. Then the watcher had to apply such simple remedies as the patient herself demanded—consisting of warm applications for the most part; Mrs. Carden preferring to endure a great amount of suffering rather than strive to deaden its intensity by opiates, which left her stupid and incapable of mental effort on the following day. Occasionally she escaped the torture, and lay silently, with large thoughtful eyes, scanning seemingly everything in the room. On these occasions the watcher spoke not.

Martha looked at the profile of the face, once so beautiful, but now sharp and attenuated, as Mrs. Carden, half raised up in the bed, leant her head on her hand. The girl wondered if she had ever loved any one very much, as she, Martha, loved Philip.

Her aunt had married an old man for money and position, when it was thought that her heart was given to one who was his junior by fifteen years. If it had been a pang to her, the suffering had been shut up in her bosom, and perhaps in that of her lover. There had never been the sully of a breath of scandal on the purity of her character or the propriety of her conduct.

The deserted lover had plunged, not into the dissipation of vice, but of commercial speculations —a more respectable gaming-table—and had been successful. He surrounded himself with the fruits of his wealth, in handsome furniture and choice paintings. It was thought that when old Mr. Carden was dead, he would realise the desire of his youth, and marry the widow; but before the old husband had been six months in his grave, and that time for speaking permitted by propriety had not arrived, a summons came from that land where there is no knowledge or device, no marrying or giving in marriage, uttered by inexorable Death. Mr. Faithful was found to have left everything he possessed to the love of his youth—perhaps also of his meridian; for though the will was dated twenty years previously to his death, when his possessions were as hundreds compared to thousands realised before his decease, he had made no other disposition of his property.

If Betsy Carden shed some natural tears at the death of her former lover, she wiped them soon—as soon, in fact, as the lawyer communicated to her the contents of the will. She did not wait for the funeral; but, on a pair of high pattens to keep her feet out of the mud, she went daily to the closed house, in which the corpse lay stark and stiff in the locked-up bedchamber, taking inventories, both literally and mentally, of all her new wealth, lest she might be defrauded of even a tittle.

Some of the furniture had been sold by auction; but the pictures and little china ornaments now decorated the oak mansion. One of these paintings Mrs. Carden had taken from *his* bedroom, and placed it in her own. It was said to be a duplicate original of that marvellous picture by De Hooge called Mors.

Nothing can be more simple or more solemn than this composition. There is no effort at picturesque forms; no arched windows with richly tinted glass. The light falls from two oblong sashes, of which the shutters of the lower frames are closed. Near the window sits a woman reading, with her back turned to the spectator. She has chosen this position that the light may fall on the book, and to avoid looking at the ghastly thing which lies covered up on the bed, the end of which only is visible. There is the pillow on the floor, which had been taken from under the head when the body had been straightened for the grave; the pair of slippers last worn by the deceased, and pushed from the side of the bed by careless feet. A picture hangs on the wall, of a funeral procession, and of the words on the book the wo-

man may read *mors*. The light flickers down, as
with a tremulous slanting movement, on the woman's cap, her apron, the floor, and the opposite
wall. She is sitting tranquilly, with a certain air
of rest from fatigue which amounts to comfort;
her feet are crossed. She reads with quiet indif-
ference as to the deceased, and only because in a
death-chamber it is the right thing to ponder on
solemn subjects. This insensibility adds to the
repose of the subject; the silence is unbroken
even by a fancied wail or a sob for the dead
man.

This painting Mrs. Carden contemplated ear-
nestly. It had been *his* favourite picture, and it
had become hers. She knew every inch of it; all
that it conveyed was present to her, though she
could not distinguish at the distance at which it
hung all the details. Probably she was running
over in her mind the circumstances connected with
her coming decease. If so, she did not shrink from
the contemplation. Of intellect originally of a
far higher class than that of her niece, each probably would have been affronted had they been
told what was the truth, that there was a strong
family likeness in their characters; Martha resembled her aunt far more than her mother. Pre-

sently Mrs. Carden turned her large eyes on her nurse.

' 'Tis a rough night seemingly,' she said; 'put back the shutters and the curtain, that I may see the sky.'

Martha did so, and Mrs. Carden looked on the moon, over which black clouds were hurrying, with edges of fleecy light. She raised herself still higher in the bed, and Martha silently arranged the pillows for her support.

The old cedar-trees creaked and dashed their spiked foliage against the windows of the inner room which looked into the garden. That in which Mrs. Carden was lying commanded the market-place. The fever which burned in her veins gave an unnatural exaltation to her thoughts. A long tremulous cry from an owl which the storm had driven from its shelter in the old garden awakened some recollections of lines learned in girlhood.

> ' Hark, the ravenne flaps hys winge
> In the briered delle belowe ;
> Hark, the deth-owl loude dothe synge
> To the nyght-mares as theie goe,'

she said. ' That "briered delle" is the Valley of the Shadow of Death. I fear it not; I shall have light in that darkness.'

She looked into the market-place, at the lamp of which the flame trembled and wavered in the gusts of the blast, and then steadied itself again into its upward movement.

'Such is faith,' said the sick woman ; 'sometimes wavering under blasts of adversity, but recovering itself, to point to heaven.'

She lay back on her pillow for about twenty minutes, and then said,

'To-morrow I must settle all I have to do. Martha, how did you live at Seadrift?'

The question was startling to the girl, who, being of a prosaic nature, and not quite understanding to what her aunt referred, said,

'On potatoes mostly.'

'Why on potatoes?'

'Because we had no money to buy meat. Sometimes we had pilchards or herrings, when they were cheap.'

'Where did your money come from?'

'I worked for it.'

'Did you like it?'

Martha was silent and sighed ; for the period of working for potatoes had latterly not been an unhappy one.

'It was not pleasant,' she said, 'to have sore

fingers and red eyes. It was rather a hard life sometimes, especially when the girls did not have new dresses on account of their fathers doing badly in trade, which was often the case.'

'Then you would like to be wealthy?'

'Yes, aunt, I should.'

'You shall be wealthy at my death, if you act according to my wishes.'

Martha looked up inquiringly, but made no response.

'I have heard that you were fool enough to engage yourself to a Catholic.'

'I am engaged to him,' said Martha, flushing with anger as she understood that her mother had betrayed her, and, as far as she could judge, against her especial warning.

'You are engaged?'

'Yes.'

'You correspond?'

'No; Philip cannot write English, so we have not heard from him.'

'Philip is his name, then?'

'Yes, aunt—Felepe Rosas; but we called him Mr. Rose.'

'He is a Catholic?'

'Yes, aunt. He was brought up by some

holy monks in a monastery on the Guadamarra range.'

'A Papist—called Philip, no doubt, after that monstrous compound of lust and bigotry, of sensuality and cruelty; a man who chose to be painted by Titian sitting at the feet of a naked shameless princess; who is represented as Adonis in the embrace of Venus, and as Actæon gazing on the uncovered forms of Diana and her nymphs; who married, against her will, his son's betrothed, and poisoned that son in prison after he had given him his blessing; who thought assassination was not murder when *he* willed it; who was the cause of torture to thousands who died in defence of their creed, the one pure belief. You are engaged, you tell me, to a Catholic called after such a king, and brought up in a convent of monks!'

Martha was silent, made so by this storm of words.

'Look,' continued her aunt, as she pointed to the lamp in the market-place, now burning clearly in a lull of the storm. 'On the spot where stands that lamp-post was Silas Carden burnt to death by Catholic and cruel men. I never could have believed that a niece of mine, who had never left her native land, never her own county even, could have come to me engaged to a Catholic. You must break this engagement.'

Martha was silent.

' 'Tis nonsense,' her aunt continued, 'to think of it, or to call it an engagement. You have not seen him or heard of him for two years.'

' A year and eight months, aunt; and he said he might be in Italy more than a year. If he is alive, he will return and marry me,' added Martha, with beautiful faith in her lover's constancy.

' How do you know he will?'

' Because,' said Martha, ' I never break my word, and I do not believe he will break his.'

' If you are to inherit my wealth, you must break your word on this occasion. My time is growing short. To-morrow I shall send instructions to Mr. Sharpin to draw up my will. You must consent to-night to be one of the greatest heiresses in the county, and give up your engagement, or be left penniless if you continue obstinately fixed on marrying a Catholic. Hark! 'tis two o'clock; your mother will come at four o'clock. There are two hours for you to turn the matter over in your mind. I will not speak to you again, except these last words, on the subject. I decide, not from any meaner motive than a deep

conviction that I am doing my duty in the determination to which I have arrived. I believe that
Mr. Marchbanks would be glad to marry you, and
I should be pleased that you should consent; but
I do not make that compulsory. Give up your
engagement, and promise never to marry a Catholic, and you will possess all my wealth, excepting a small annuity to your mother, which, you
understand, is *for her only*, and will cease at her
death. No money of mine shall go to a Papist.'

'Aunt!' said Martha; but Mrs. Carden turned
over on her pillow, and declined by a gesture to
hear anything her niece was about to say.

Martha remained quietly looking into the market-place, and watching the clouds that hurried
over the moon. She felt, without being able to
reason on the subject, that her aunt was wrong.
She knew that the mode of life which she had
led for a year and eight months would make her
return to her former poverty more irksome. O,
if her mother had not betrayed her, perhaps her
aunt would never have known the fact of her engagement, and would have left her money enough
to make Philip a rich man! How happy she
would have been to have endowed him with abundant wealth!

Then she reproached herself with the wish to have obtained opulence under false pretences. Her thoughts wandered to Mr. Marchbanks— could it be true that he wished to marry her? A pleased smile spread over the heavy expression of her face, and lightened it for a moment; for no woman is insensible to such a compliment to her attractions.

The question between the two religions did not affect her in the least. She and her mother were Methodists really, though they had attended church since they had lived at the oak house. Philip was a Catholic, but he had been, like his religion, beaten down by stronger power—he by raging of the storm, his Church by 'the madness of the people.' He had come helpless, and only not a suppliant because his feebleness was dumb and akin to death. A Catholic was, to the mind of Mrs. Carden, personified by Lord Rich, mounted on a powerful horse, which rears when his rider urges him onward to get a better view of the martyr slowly consuming amongst green fagots, whilst the Catholic peer hissed out his words of scoffing and vituperation against the Protestant religion and its victim.

Martha saw only the pale exhausted body of

her beloved lying in a helpless heap in her path; the languor of semi-death in his half-closed eyes, the utter powerlessness to aid himself shown in each flaccid limb. Both women were right from their points of view. The aunt judged Catholicism as it had been; the niece had been taught by love to consider it as it was.

When the church-clock chimed three and three-quarters, Mrs. Carden turned her large hollow eyes on Martha, and asked,

'Well?'

'Yes, aunt,' said Martha timidly; for she was grieved to vex a dying woman.

'Have you decided?'

'I have never wavered, aunt; I will never give up Philip. I am sorry he is a Catholic, since it vexes you; but probably he is as fond of his faith as we are of ours, and I should think nothing of him if he gave it up for money; for what shall a man profit if he gain the whole world, and lose his own soul?'

'Then you think he is right, I suppose?'

'I do not know that he is wrong, and I do know that it would be wicked to change for the sake of money. I am not clever, aunt, as you are, and I cannot talk as you do; but I have learnt to be true and just in all my dealings. I told Philip I would marry him, and I mean to wait for his return.'

'How do you mean to live when your mother dies, if this man does not return?'

'I will do what I did for ten years, when I did not know whether you were alive or dead, aunt; when I supported my mother and myself by hard work. And if I could bear the pinching of poverty for her, I suppose I can bear it for myself; and if I cannot bear it, I can but die, and small moan made.'

There was something defiant in the tone of the niece, and unswerving resolution reigned in the breast of the invalid.

'Very well,' said Mrs. Carden. 'That is settled, and we need not recur to it again.'

At four o'clock Mrs. Clemens came in in her dressing-gown and night-cap to complete the remainder of the watch. The conversation with Martha had increased the fever in her aunt's frame, and for an hour Nancy strove all her feeble efforts to alleviate the fearful torture which drew stifled groans from the sick woman. Mrs. Clemens ministered to her with tears streaming over her little withered old cheeks.

'O Betsy, if I could but bear it for you just one half-hour!' she sobbed.

'It would come harder on you, sister; you are so gentle. But 'tis better now. There, now I shall sleep. Lie down by my side, Nancy.'

And the patient held the hand of her sister, and bore without any movement than a closer grasp the return of the paroxysm, pleased that the tear-charged eyelids of the elder woman were closed in sleep. By degrees the torture subsided as the beams of the first dawn of morning stole into the chamber, scaring away, as it were, all the phantoms of evil and suffering which had floated like incubi in the shadows of night.

In the morning, Mrs. Carden sent for Mr. Sharpin, the attorney, who was in consultation with her alone for some time. On leaving the apartment, he bowed slightly to Mrs. Clemens, but did not honour Martha with any salutation.

Mrs. Clemens looked anxiously at her sister on returning to the bedroom after his departure. Her expression said, if ever looks could speak, You haven't been unkind to poor Martha? But there was no answering glance in Betsy's face; and Mrs. Clemens, easily diverted from her own train of thought by the exhibition of suffering in another, felt such pity for the exhaustion visible in the countenance of her sister, that she set to work to concoct some of that beef-tea for which she was so celebrated, and which might have worked wonders had the patients ever been persuaded to swallow more than a few spoonfuls of it.

CHAPTER XXI.

‘ We take cunning for a sinister or crooked wisdom.’
BACON.

MARTHA was glad when she was free to escape from the bedchamber of her aunt. Mrs. Carden never referred again to the subject ; but Martha felt as a criminal in her presence, and was less adroit in the shifting of pillows and the smoothing of sheets in consequence. Mrs. Clemens was ever ready to take her daughter's place. Those young things, she would say, want air and exercise — forgetting that Martha was not so very young a thing, having reached twenty-nine years of age.

Martha had penetrated to the garden of the

empty house on one or two occasions, but it seemed
unoccupied no longer. Carpenters were sawing,
bricklayers ascending tall ladders with heavy hods
of mortar on their heads and trowels in hand;
then came painters and paper-hangers; and Martha took some interest in all their proceedings, as
do folks whose mental powers are limited, and
who have no intellectual resources to carry them
out of the present time. These doings made,
moreover, a subject of conversation when she sat
with her mother over their lonely meals; and the
difficulty felt by the paper-hangers of getting
enough of a selected pattern of paper to cover the
drawing-room which a stranger was to inhabit, was,
in the sadness and vacuity of their lives, quite
something worthy of thought and anxiety.

At length the decoration of the house was
completed, and there was a lull. Then strange
servants were to be seen peering into the deserted
garden, but too busy to stray into it. When they
arrived, Martha withdrew to the avenue, and
walked no longer in the garden. One day, as
she strolled listlessly in the month of November
under the elms, she saw a young female with two
little children running before her. The stranger
looked up, and seeing a lady in a handsome chin-

chilla muff and tippet, began to wriggle in her progress as if she were the serpent of old Nile.

'And by her gait the Queen of Love is known,'

says Dryden.

''Tis Julia Deal, by her walk,' said Martha. 'What a pity she does not move along like a Christian, and not a snake!'

The women met midway in the avenue. Martha was the first to speak, for she had recognised the old affectation which disfigured a very pretty girl. All Julia's attention had been absorbed by the splendour of the muff and tippet. 'That cost —let me see,' said Julia to herself; 'well, from fifteen to twenty pounds. Pa never had so handsome a one; it beats Mrs. Bolitho's.' The possessor of such treasures must be worth the exhibition of a little affectation; so Julia went through her usual antics to attract attention and, as she believed, admiration, and was greatly astonished when a serene face above the tippet said,

'Julia! Miss Deal!'

'Why, Martha Clemens! how stupid of me not to know you! But, my dear, you are grown quite stout; you look so well; really quite plumped out. I might have remembered that you were

living here; but I was not thinking about you at
the moment we met. To tell the truth, that fur
riveted my gaze.'

'But how—' said Martha, and stopped, for she
thought she was impertinent.

'Yes; how got I here?' said Julia.—'Eva
and George, now go to the end of the avenue,
you, and see which can reach the other end first.
—Little pitchers, my dear,' exclaimed the young
lady as they went off. 'Now I'll tell you all
about it. You see, it was horridly dull at home,

> "To pass my time with reading and bohea,
>   And sip and spill my solitary tea."

I got so sick of it; no chance of anything to see or
do. Your young man was a godsend for a little
time; but such lucky things don't happen every
day. We had another shipwreck last winter,—a
grand one; *two* men were washed up, or scrambled
up. They were taken in and made much of, and
Emma Damnall and I went to see them, to offer
some religious consolation—at least, *she* did; caught
it from her pa, I should say. Well, my dear,
they were coarse middle-aged men, with no eyes
to speak of, who could not understand a word of
French—at least not *my* French, nor Emma's; and
they did nothing but smoke long pipes and drink

gin; for the folks pitied them so much for the
quantity of salt water they had been compelled
to swallow, that first one and then the other gave
them spirits and tobacco, so that they were incapable of doing anything but lie on some trusses
of straw before night came. Not a bit like your
shipwrecked hero; such a beauty he was! Heard
from him lately?

"As the bolt bursts on high from the black cloud that bound
it,
Burst the soul of that eye from the long lashes round it." '

'But,' interrupted Martha, 'you have not told
me how you came here.'

'O, I forgot. Yes, I'll tell you. I was so
clever—so crafty. You know Lord Tynedale was
down at the Queen of the East's. He came to
our shop one day, and he looked at me as if he
thought I was a pretty girl. That brazened me
up to ask a favour; but pa was in the shop, and
I could not say anything then to my lord, and I
never chanced to see him again. So I took up
one of pa's best shawls, and said, "Father, I want
this shawl for my own as a birthday present."
"All right," said he; "but 'tis not due yet."
But I took it without more ado, and up I went
to Mrs. Bolitho's. "Mrs. B.," said I, "you've been

a good customer to our shop, and pa sends you this little present; and I think you'll own 'tis a handsome shawl;" and I shook out the shawl over the back of the great chair. "Miss Deal," said she, "your pa overwhelms me so, that I don't know how to look." And for all that, she did know which way to look; for she turned herself behind and before at the looking-glass to see how she looked, and then she said with a broad grin, "And what can I do for your pa, my dear?" Says I, quite solemn, "Mrs. B., I want you to speak to Lord Tynedale to get me the place of nursery governess to some nice lady, where there are not too many children. His lordship knows me by sight," said I, "and if *you* would speak for me, Mrs. B., the business would be done." Well, my dear, the business *was* done. Lord Tynedale spoke to his young cousin, who has a friend who wanted a governess. Here I am. Those are my pupils. Their ma is. coming in a day or two. We were sent down here because Mrs. Ashhurst was going on a visit somewhere. I don't much care whether she is here or away; she does not interfere with me.'

'I think I saw the lady, Mrs. Ashhurst, in the garden here when she came to look at the house, and another younger person.'

'Ah, yes; that was the young cousin or grand-niece of my lord's. She has been staying with her friend Mrs. Ashhurst.'

'And where is she now?' said Martha uneasily.

'Lor'! my dear, how can I tell? I'll find out, if you want her address. But did you have a good view of her?'

'Yes.'

'Then did you ever see anything so exquisite as the set of her skirt? I wanted some one clever in dress-making to look well at it. *I* believe that the whole dress is cut on the cross.'

'I did not see her frock,' said Martha sadly; 'I only looked at her beautiful face.'

'She's well to look at, no doubt; though, for *my* part, I think there is nothing to equal a dark beauty.

> " Her eyes' dark charms 'twere vain to tell ;
> But gaze on those of the gazelle,
> So clear, so languishingly dark." '

Julia thought this description applicable to herself, and repeated it with unction. 'But this is not complimentary to you, Martha my dear,' she added affectedly.

'I am not a beauty, and never pretended to be one,' said Martha doggedly.

'Not when your picture was painted, eh?' said Julia with a touch of spite.

Martha blushed and said nothing.

Certainly Julia had not forgotten

> 'To shoot out her tongue like arrows,
> Even bitter words.'

On these occasions Martha could only suffer; she had not sufficient quickness to retaliate.

The interview was becoming painful to Martha, when it was interrupted by the children, who came like a mighty rushing wind, and flung themselves against the two young women in the anxiety to outstrip each other.

''Tis dinner-time,' said one.

'I must go in now, Martha my dear. These children must be attended to and fed. I hope we shall meet again soon, and then you must tell me all about yourself. Give my regards to your mother,' she said patronisingly as she went off.

Julia Deal had told part, but not all, of her doings and motives. She had been wrought to desperation by the fact, which each day became more patent, that she was unsought, and that, as she said,

> 'Her lonely unappropriated sweets
> Shone like a cowslip on some craggy steep,
> Not to be come at by the willing hand;'

for the simple reason that no hand was there, willing or unwilling, to approach the beautiful blossom.

When a youth arrived at years of indiscretion in Seadrift, and had to be taught to learn and labour truly to gain his own living, and to do his duty in this state of life, his parents sent him away, because in a village so comatose as Seadrift there was no awakening, with any prospect of success, for any undertaking. The place suffered from an insensibility akin to dissolution. The result was, that the young men formed attachments in new localities, and the maidens remained unwedded at home.

CHAPTER XXII.

' Do you take me for a Roman matron,
Bred tamely to the spindle and the loom ?'

A. PHILIPS.

WHEN Dr. Mereside's uncle had arrived at Seadrift, great had been the agitation in spinsterian breasts. The single ladies of doubtful—that is, of middle—age pulled out intrusive gray hairs, sponged their faded silks, and dyed their faded ribbons and retrimmed with them their shabby bonnets.

Before his arrival, Julia had decided, that to be the wife of a wealthy old man would be far pleasanter than remaining Julia Deal. She longed to go to London and see theatres, and wear smart dresses, and attend balls. She was buried in Seadrift.

She induced her father to call on Mr. Mereside, and ask him to come and play a game of whist in the evening. Mrs. Mereside, the doctor's wife, looked very grave when she found the invitation had been given and accepted. Mr. Mereside had found his leisure irksome as he began to recover his health, and the prospect of a game of whist was not disagreeable. Julia, alas, was not a whist-player, and an old widow-lady was invited to make a fourth.

The snug room had the green table, two silver candlesticks, several packs of cards, and a mother-of-pearl carved box with rich pink-silk lining, and filled with glittering fishes, circles, oblongs, and squares, all of mother-of-pearl, shining with wavering light; which had been objects of awe and desire to Julia when a baby, but the use of which she had never before divined. For 'terrors of the Lord,' as Mr. Damnall had said, but really terrors of the fulminations of that energetic pastor, had for fifteen years banished the card-table and its painted packs to a back room, where it innocently supported a jar of potpourri. Mrs. Deal had found her husband disposed to be gay when they were first married, and the dissenting parson had been called in in aid of the uxorian authority; and together they kept young Mr. Deal within bounds.

But the bounds which were useful in restraining the wanderings of a newly-married man became inconveniently limited when Julia grew up and had to be presented to society. Mrs. Deal no longer feared that her husband would go out to the public-house at night for the enjoyment of smoking, forbidden at home. He had outgrown those temptations; and it was time now to give him a little indulgence in his own house, at his time of life, as Mrs. Deal had said sweetly. So the card-party was a treat to her husband, an act of hospitality to a wealthy London merchant, and 'an opening' for her darling Julia.

The evening arrived; the unconscious victim arrived also in the fly from Mrs. Bolitho's, for his feet were hardly in trim to encounter the flints of Seadrift. He emerged from the narrow staircase into the blaze of the four wax-candles and Julia's flashing eyes at the same moment; but seated himself in silent composure whilst coffee was administered to him by Julia herself, and the cream added lavishly, as is usual with the member of the family who doesn't pay for it. But like a dog who watches the bone which is to come to him, though he is too well-bred to ask for it, Mr. Mereside's thoughts were turned towards the whist-table. His eyes sought impatiently the hands of the elderly widow-lady, who was playing with her teaspoon in a manner distracting to a nervous fidgety man.

'Why don't she drink it and let us begin?' he was thinking. Then a sudden hope brightened his eyes, and raising them to the face of Julia, he said with eagerness, 'Perhaps *you* play whist?' Julia smiled, and said, 'O no!' and dropped her head first on the right and then on the left shoulder, and moved her body in an eel-like manner from her hips; to all of which the guest responded by an impatient grunt; and Mrs. Deal, seeing symptoms of discontent, proceeded to cut the cards, she and her husband playing together, and the widow and Mr. Mereside.

Then, as the candles showed the bald heads of both gentlemen, Julia looked on, leaning her finger-tips on the back of her papa's chair, and watching with feigned interest Mr. Mereside's game, to judge whether or not he was winning. He never thought of her except as an unnecessary person in the room. His complaisance to the weaker sex was not great. He reproved the widow for making a revoke in bitter terms, and brought tears into her weather-beaten eyelids. Julia, finding that 'his most tender mercy was neglect,' declared afterwards to her mother that he was an old brute, and that she would not marry him if he was decked in diamonds. She was going to bed without waiting for the supper of roast ducks and apple-tarts, when Emma Damnall walked in uninvited, and saw all the atrocities going on in the drawing-room of members of her father's congregation.

She had suspected something of the sort, and the groan she gave was dreadful; but she had on a becoming bonnet, and drew up near the table of abominations, where the light could fall on her pretty fair face. If such disgraceful acts of gambling were perpetrated, why should she not have her chance as well as another? Indeed, so pleased was she by one or two glances given her by the London merchant, that she accepted the invitation

Mrs. Deal gave her to stay to supper, in the hope of propitiating the minister's daughter; and, worse and worse, Mr. Meredith, who was in high spirits at having won thirty shillings from his host and hostess, offered to drop her at her own door in his fly.

The looks exchanged by mother and daughter, when the merchant and the minister's daughter drove off together, spoke volumes of mortification and concealed wrath.

'He shall never enter *my* doors again!' said the angry mother. And the next day Julia presented her imitation cashmere, which resulted in her present engagement. It was true that she had thus left the coast clear for Miss Damnall; but she wisely imagined, that the wealthy London merchant would not be attracted by threats of divine vengeance when he had been insensible of the attractions of a seraph.

Miss Damnall, however, created some sensation in the mind of the old gentleman, and Mrs. Mereside was uneasy thereat; but a timely fit of the gout brought him to his senses, and the chances of the doctor's heirship seemed to depend now on his own length of life.

CHAPTER XXIII.

*'And thy life shall hang in doubt before thee, and thou shalt
fear day and night.'*

MARTHA kept clear of the avenue for some
time, from a nervous dread that Julia should catch
her and inquire about Philip.   One day, on looking into the garden of her aunt's house, she saw
that lively young woman making signs to her to
come down; and obeyed, lest Ruth should see the
intruder, and report to Mrs. Carden of the incursion.   Martha's aunt, when she had settled her
affairs by aid of the lawyer, rallied considerably;
suffering less from fever and pain, and regaining
partially her appetite.   Thus time had crept on, to
the first week in December, with little alteration
in the state of affairs at the Oak House.

'Well, Martha,' said the cheerful young female,
'I must say you have kept yourself pretty close.

> " Caged in old woods where reverend echoes wake,
>   Her little soul all panting to be free;
>   Nor moved by prayers, nor to be moved by tears."

Aunt would not let you out, eh?   I thought I
would go up to the fortress and summon it to
surrender; and here you are!   Well, I thought I
would let you know that my holidays begin to-

morrow, and I am going back to Seadrift for a
month. Any message to the old place? If Mr.
Rose goes back there to look for you, I will put
him in my pocket, metaphorically, and keep him
for you. I rather want to see how Emma Damnall gets on. Do you know, that girl has managed
lately to look too pretty for my peace of mind.'

'I should not have suspected that,' said Martha, with a slow smile which was complimentary to
Julia's looks.

> 'O happy fair, thine eyes are loadstars!'

exclaimed Julia.

'I'm sorry to confess 'tis true, my dear, and I
owe her a grudge. See if I don't pay it off some
day—a nasty thing! But I have no time; I must
go back. Shall I give your remembrances to the
folks there? I shall not forget to say how hand-
somely you are dressed, and all the world says
you are the heiress of your aunt's great wealth.'

'I am not,' replied Martha briefly.

'Ha, ha! you won't make me believe that. Ta-
ta, my dear. See you again in a month's time.'

Martha was not sorry that she had left the
avenue free for her uninterrupted walks. The
cold gray life she led went on without variety,

excepting that given by her walks during a certain portion of the day.

Her Cornish habit of disregarding drizzling rain made her take exercise in a rough cloak belonging to her mother, which had been brought from Seadrift; with that, in a shabby bonnet, she used to walk up and down the elm-avenue, with no dread of being seen by any one.

Martha in this costume, if it must be confessed, looked as stout as her mother. In it her charms of fairness, plumpness, and smoothness were obscured, and only added to a general clumsiness of appearance.

She had one afternoon just turned to go down the avenue, when she heard a chorus of laughter and little shrieks, either of anxiety or amusement, behind her. She began to walk a little faster, without turning her head, not wishing to be seen. Then for a space the voices died away in the distance, and she had nearly reached the gate of her aunt's garden, when a heavy bird swooped suddenly and settled on Martha's bonnet, which he began to tear, shrieking and flapping his wings in a manner most perplexing and alarming to the sufferer.

Martha's slowness stood her friend. She showed

neither terror nor disturbance, though the beak of the creature was tearing off the broken fragments of her straw bonnet, as if he meant to pierce into her brain. She knew the bonnet was of little consequence; and putting up her hand softly to where she felt the claws of the bird, she had the satisfaction of feeling the rough white feet of the assailant placed on one of her fingers, and removed to make room for the other, till the bird had travelled down, first to her shoulder and then to the bend of her arm, revealing a beautiful creature of the parrot tribe, with gray feathers, but breasted with brilliant pink. He seemed satisfied with his position, giving sundry little clucks with his tongue against his beak, and eyeing her curiously, attracted, perhaps, by her immobility.

Martha turned to where she had heard the wild laughter and small shrieks, which she now understood to have arisen from women and children in pursuit of a stray captive. She was nailed to the spot, understanding that it would be discourteous to allow the bird to escape or to carry him off.

One figure was in advance of the rest. She ran forward, looking up as she came, to scrutinise the branches for the truant. She had no hat or cloak on, and her opulence of hair floated back as she ran forward, bounding over the dead foliage, crisp with frost. Martha's heart beat thick with the doubt whether the young beauty would recognise her old schoolfellow. As she approached nearer, Martha's eyes fell on the group following the young lady at a considerable distance. It was composed of Julia's two pupils and a gentleman, whose appearance so riveted Martha's gaze, that she scarcely heard the silvery tones of the young lady's voice, and did not in the least understand what she said. He looked like Philip, Martha thought.

One of the children had caught her foot in the broken branch of a tree, and had fallen, and the gentleman was stooping over her, raising and seemingly striving to console her. But though her loving instinct pointed out her beloved, reason told Martha that the man she was observing was taller, darker, and more developed than her affianced husband. He was still stooping over the child when the beauty reiterated her thanks to Martha, her condolences as to the destruction of the bonnet, and her offers to relieve her from farther charge of the bird, holding out her hand to receive him at the same time. Martha held up her arm, and the young lady passed a silver chain through a ring attached to his leg, and carried him off, with a smiling bow to Martha.

. She had not recognised Martha, in whom twelve years had made considerable alteration, and whom she had never much noticed when living in Miss Wise's school. *She* had been the one object of universal homage and attention, and the presence of Martha had been unobserved amongst a bevy of girls whom she had been taught to consider her inferiors.

She had been perfectly well-bred and polite in her thanks to Martha, whom she took for a stranger, when she had repossessed herself of the bird. Martha's eyes were fixed on the gentleman, who was following the path down the avenue to meet the young lady on her return as fast as he could; for his feet were impeded by the steps of the child, who hung, with her hand in his, weeping, and with the other wiping the tears from her eyes. His eyes were flashing with eager joy, and Martha heard him say,

'You have got him?'

The lady answered, and they walked together slowly back to their own domain, followed by the children.

CHAPTER XXIV.

O, how thou hast with jealousy infected
The sweetness of affiance !'

SHAKESPEARE.

MARTHA felt her head turn giddy. The voice was like that of Philip, but the perfect pronunciation of English was unlike that formed by his stammering tongue before he left Seadrift. She felt sick with the flutter of agitation and apprehension in her heart.

She returned to the house, and leaving her ragged bonnet and rough cloak in her bedroom, she joined her mother, who was sitting in the drawing-room overlooking the square.

'Martha, look here! Quick, come at once !'

A handsome carriage and four fine horses, with footmen and coachman dressed in the Tynedale livery, were at the door of the Cedar House —for it was called thus in contradistinction to the Oak House.

Just as Martha reached the window, a young lady stepped into the carriage, followed by a tall dark gentleman. The door was shut, the horses sprang forward, and the equipage disappeared.

Mrs. Clemens looked pale, as she turned and saw Martha's pallid face.

'My dear,' said the mother, 'it may be fancy, but I saw them get out an hour ago, and I could not help thinking—I daresay it is not so really, you know—that it seemed to me as if the gentleman had a look of Mr. Rose. 'Tis Lord Tynedale's livery, you see.'

Martha said nothing in reply. She turned her head away, and took up her work-basket. Her mother knew her moods too well to speak to her. All that day and night Martha's feelings were like a lava-flood; but no one could guess it in her silence and seeming repose of manner. The irritation of her feelings made her life a misery to her. She felt as if she could not sit still, when stillness was imperative to the comfort of the invalid.

She would try to make certain next day, if she could see those little children walking in the avenue. She became as eager for the flight of Time as if she should escape a great evil on his wings. She thought it was certainly Philip; but could he be in England, and not have communicated with her? It was two years now since they first met. Perhaps it was not Philip after all; this man spoke so distinctly and without any accent.

The idea that it had not been Philip was a comfort to her, but one which was shaken again as she sat at breakfast with her mother, who could not help saying what was in her mind.

'I should not have thought so much about its being Philip,' she began suddenly, 'only the gentleman took a picture framed from the carriage, and would not let the footman touch it; and as he put it under his arm, and held his other hand to help the young lady out, the action seemed so like what I used to see in Mr. Rose so often at home.'

'I don't think it was Philip, mother,' said Martha quietly. 'We should have heard from him, had he been in England.'

'Ah,' replied Mrs. Clemens; 'but he could not write much, or, indeed, at all, my dear; so it would not be very extraordinary if he has not written; and, poor fellow, you know he is not his own master. I daresay he is under my lord's orders, if he is in England, and he will be sure to come forward sooner or later, Martha; for if I ever saw a poor young man in love, he was so with you, my dear.'

Martha had a wan smile on her face at her mother's speech. It comforted her, for she knew nothing of love except what she felt herself; and her mother must know, because she had been married.

Thus argued this simple-minded young woman. Julia Deal would never have been so ignorant as to suppose love and marriage were inseparable.

The next day after the apparition of the gentleman and lady, Martha went to the avenue; and presently, seeing the little girls walking hand-in-hand in a dreary vacuity of amusement, she went to make herself agreeable to them, and find out the name of the gentleman who had called on the previous day. She began by pitying one of the little girls for having a piece of sticking-plaster on her forehead.

'You hurt yourself yesterday?'

'Ye-es,' said the girl, beginning to sob again.

'You fell down, and a kind gentleman picked you up?' said Martha tentatively.

A sob was the only audible answer; and now the elder girl, looking very prim, said to Martha:

'Are you a housekeeper? Because we are told we are not to speak to queer-looking people or servants; and a housekeeper is a servant, is she not?'

'I am not a housekeeper. Why do you think I am?'

'Only because when Geniveve came back with the bird, Mr. Ose said, "How did you get it again?" and she answered, "There was a respectable middle-aged woman at the end of the avenue, who looks like a housekeeper; she caught the bird, and kept it till I reached her."'

Inexpressibly mortified by the words so innocently repeated by the child, Martha felt inclined to leave them without another sentence; but there were too many phantoms of suffering in that dreary mansion to encounter again, without the power of dispelling them by that magic word 'certainty.'

'Do you like Mr. Ose very much?'

'Yes.'

'Does he speak English?'

The child's large eyes opened wider at the question, as she replied,

'Why not?'

'O, I thought he was a foreign gentleman,' said Martha apologetically. 'Have you known him long?'

'No,' said the little child.

'Only yesterday,' said the other; 'he came in a ship—a great way off.'

'And where is he now?' asked Martha breathlessly.

'Don't know,' the children said.

'Did he bring a picture?' said the woman, hungry for information of her beloved.

'O, such a pretty picture! Two ladies, and one putting a ring on a little baby's finger; and such a beautiful frame!' said the younger child. 'Mr. Ose brought it for mamma,' added the latter, with a look of importance.

'His name is not *Ose*,' said the elder; 'you can't speak plain; you talk like a baby.'

'What is his name, then?' said Martha.

'Felepe Rosas,' said the elder grandly. 'He is a Spanish gentleman.'

'Does Lord Tynedale live in this county.'

'I don't know,' said the younger.

'I know all about counties,' said the elder; 'fifty-two in England and Wales; that's in my lesson to-day. Six to the north, nine to the east, twelve to the west, ten to the south, and fifteen in the middle,' glibly repeated she.

'And in which of all these does Lord Tynedale live?'

'O, mamma says he has several places; I don't know where.'

'Is it a great way off?'

'I suppose not, as Geniveve and Mr. Rose came yesterday and went back again.'

Martha walked silently by the side of the children till they came to the garden-door, which they were about to enter. The elder girl was so thoughtful, that Martha asked if anything vexed her.

'I was thinking,' said the child, 'if I ought to tell mamma that I have been talking to—anybody.'

Martha flushed.

'You had better tell your mamma the truth: you may say that you spoke to the niece of the lady who lives in the other house like your own, called the Oak House; and that she knows your governess, Miss Deal, intimately.' And poor Martha, having vouched for her respectability in the best manner she could, returned home very crestfallen at the consciousness of the undignified step she had taken in cross-questioning the children. She felt like a patient with an angry wound, who cannot bear a finger near it.

This was the state of her mind, and she shrank from the thought of telling her mother what she had just ascertained—that Philip was within a few miles of them. Her mother's vague and inane efforts at consolation, however well intended, were irritating instead of soothing. Martha felt that at present she could not bear them.

'When I get better, I can tell her; when something is done, something decided happens; not just now. I cannot bear her talking about it, and speculating as to whether Philip has forgotten me. Aunt said he had; of all the things she said, that was what hurt most. I did not so much mind about her leaving the money away from me. If he has forgotten me, what can I do? I can die— yes; but I must kill myself to do that. I am so strong, nothing but violence will kill me. O, Philip, you *must* not desert me. I *cannot* bear it!'

She heard no more of Philip. The little girls no longer frequented the avenue, and Martha felt snubbed by a circumstance which might, after all, have proved unintentional. She did not know whether Julia Deal had resumed her duties; if so, the whole family were away probably, for she felt that Julia would have found her out, if only to gratify her own love of talking. She fancied by the appearance of the Cedar House that its windows were closed, at least those which looked into the square. The weather was so severe, however, that it was unlikely that the sashes should be open if the family were at home. She never went into the street, so that she could not satisfy herself entirely on this point.

CHAPTER XXV.

'When the light of life is waning,
  Weep not for me;
When the filmy eye is straining,
  Weep not for me;
When the languid pulse is ceasing—
Start not for its swift decreasing,
'Tis the fetter'd soul's releasing—
  Weep not for me.'

THE end of March arrived, and each day Martha's hopes grew less. Her occupations now, however, were too urgent to admit of the indulgence of selfish sorrows or of sentimental repinings. In the presence of great bodily agony, nothing seems so overwhelming as its contemplation; all else fades into insignificance when we witness the slow resolving of life into corruption — life not ebbing by gentle and sleepy subsidence, but fighting inch by inch against the dull encroachment of death. Mrs. Carden had been so full of bodily energy, that it seemed as if its extinction was unusually delayed, and at the price of greater suffering than usual. She refused medical aid, declaring that doctors were useless in her complaint, and that she would not go out of the world in a state of intoxication from opiates.

'What suffering nature chooses to inflict, I must bear,' she would say; 'but how do we know the frightful agony in the brain of those who take the comforting poppy - juice day after day and night after night, till the reeling mind is terrified by visions and disquieted by dreams, and sinks into death in the terror and confusion of being pursued by formless phantoms urging it to unknown depths of horror?'

She was reduced to the appearance of a skeleton now, and took only a small quantity of bread-and-milk daily. The service of the day was read by her sofa every morning still, and every evening Mr. Marchbanks called with his bundle of letters.

On this day Martha stole down and told him that she did not think Mrs. Carden was capable of attending any longer to business. Her mind had wandered occasionally during the previous night, disturbed seemingly by the intensity of her pain; all the sufferings undergone by Silas Carden seemed present to her imagination, which was highly wrought by the fever hurrying through her veins.

No visits from the clergyman of the parish had been sought for or desired by Mrs. Carden during her long decline.

'Would a farmer be so mad,' she would say, 'as to send for a clergyman to pray for abundant crops when the sickle is at the wheat? As they have grown, so will the produce be. What ye have sowed, that shall ye also reap.'

Mrs. Clemens, timid and terrified, longed to have some pious words uttered over the death-bed by the good gentleman who lived at the vicarage; but Martha forbade anything to be done which had not her aunt's sanction. Mrs. Carden had been wont to say, 'Are we more merciful than God, that we should entreat Him to show mercy? Are we so much wiser than He, that we know what is best for us? Is He, with whom there is no changeableness nor shadow of turning, to be dissuaded from His immutable decrees by our entreaties? And if so, shall these entreaties be put off till the eye is dim, and the tongue stiffening in death?'

So no sounds interrupted the repose of the death-bed, excepting the expressions of suffering, which became more urgent as the mental power which had restrained their utterance grew less.

Now, as the dull evening drew on, the mind
dwelt on the martyrdom of Silas Carden. She
had tried to bear her agony, thinking of the pangs
he had sustained in testimony of the truth. She
had shown the greatest anxiety that the bill going
through the Lower House of Parliament should
not pass, and had been lavish in her subscriptions
for the election of members likely to oppose the
measure.

As the twilight drew on, Mrs. Clemens, Martha, and Ruth sat silently in the bedchamber of
the dying woman. The sky was heavy with clouds
on that bleak evening in April; and only a
distant hum of confused life was heard in the
town, through which the hurry of occupation was
subsiding.

They heard a sound from the bed.

'O, that I might die at once!' murmured Mrs.
Carden, in the intervals of her agony. 'This room
is suffocating. *He* could scarce draw his breath
for the cruel creeping flames. Open the window!
put aside the curtain! support me!'

Martha crept up by the tester of the bed, and
raised her aunt's shoulders, supporting them on
her knees. Mrs. Carden turned her head to feel
once more the cool breeze of night play on her fore-

head, in which the veins showed, knotted from the hot
blood which distended them. Her large thoughtful eyes seemed to search into the darkness, as if
to divine where might be the path her disembodied
spirit would soon pass over. As she gazed into the
gloom, a sudden light illuminated the market-place
and flushed with a red glare the sky, in its red
radiance flinging into insignificance the quiet lamp,
whose light was unvarying. A loud hurrah burst
from a hundred voices, as the flames leapt up, and
the tar-barrels ran over with liquid fire.

'What means this? Have they another martyr to burn? Do they this in mockery of that
victim of Catholicism, Silas Carden?' said the sick
woman.

' 'Tis a bonfire,' said Ruth.

'On what occasion?' asked her mistress.

There was no answer from the three women
who surrounded the dying woman; and as she
leant on her elbow, with her eyes fixed on the
blazing light, a voice in the crowd cried out,

'Catholic Emancipation! Majority one hundred and seventy-eight! Hurrah!'

The voices rose and sank in repeated acclama-
tion, so that no other sounds were audible.

At length there was a lull; and Mrs. Carden

sought with her looks where the light of the
lamp was still visible to her eyes, accustomed to
seek for it nightly.

'The morning cometh, saith the watchman,'
she murmured; 'also the night;' and her eyes
closed, never to be opened again.

Martha believed that she was dead from the
weight on her knees, which ached now from the
constraint of her position.

'Mother,' she said softly, for the fitful light
made by the rising and falling of the bonfire made
a ghastly illumination in the death-chamber,—
'mother, will you not strike a light?'

'I am afraid it will disturb your aunt, my dear,'
the mother replied in a whisper.

'No, mother; it will not disturb her.'

There was an inflection in Martha's voice,
which told the state of the departed; and Ruth
hurried away to procure lights; and then the two
elder women paid the last offices of duty and affection to the deceased.

'Some one must order the coffin,' said Mrs.
Clemens, in a whisper to Ruth.

'No occasion,' replied that faithful servant.
'My mistress has had one for the last two years
in the outhouse downstairs leading into the gar-

den. She was a lady who liked to do everything for herself whilst she lived, and as much as she could after her death. So that is not to do.'

The tears which fell for the deceased were shed by Mrs. Clemens and Ruth. Martha had none to give. All joy and all sorrow were alike to her in the dull haze of uncertainty which clouded her mind as to her lover's constancy.

CHAPTER XVI.

'I come to wive it wealthily in Padua.'
SHAKESPEARE.

ON the following day Mr. Marchbanks called and asked if the ladies would see him, and suggested when he was admitted that Mrs. Carden's will should be sought for, and Mr. Sharpin invited to read it, as it might contain orders with regard to the funeral. Martha answered that it needed not to be looked for, as her aunt had told her where to seek for it. Mr. Sharpin had placed it on the dressing-table; and Martha, coming with a cup of tea in her hand, had pushed it aside to make room, and had been told by her aunt what it was.

'I believe,' said the merchant, 'I am one of the

trustees and executors; but I don't know with whom I am associated. Mrs. Carden asked if I would consent to act.'

Mr. Marchbanks did not say (what he thought) that probably he should have a thousand pounds left him for his trouble.

On the next morning Mr. Sharpin assembled the servants, with Mrs. Clemens and Mr. Marchbanks. Martha followed listlessly, though uninvited.

After specifying sums left to different servants, according to their length of servitude, and willing one hundred pounds a year, free of legacy-duty, to Ruth Roothing, she bequeathed an annuity of three hundred per annum to her sister Ann or Nancy Clemens of Seadrift, and all the residue of her enormous property to Mr. Marchbanks; with a wish that her sister should occupy the Oak House without any derangement of the furniture so long as she desired to remain there, and till it might be convenient for her to return to Seadrift. Nothing was said with regard to Martha.

The countenance of Mr. Marchbanks had been very sad but tranquil when Mr. Sharpin began to read; nor was he much disturbed when he heard that he was to have the whole of this enormous wealth, waiting for the words 'in trust for'; but when he found himself the sole possessor, with the exception of a few minor legacies and the annuities to Mrs. Clemens and to Ruth, he could scarcely believe the evidence of his ears.

He was awakened from his reverie by the voice of Mr. Sharpin in congratulation.

'Really, this takes me so much by surprise, I cannot tell what to say,' said he; and he stole a look at Martha, whose face wore her habitual expression of tranquil sadness, but none of anger, displeasure, or disappointment.

'She believes that I love her, and that it will be all one whether the money is hers or mine,' was the not unnatural idea that seemed to elucidate the mystery to the mind of Mr. Marchbanks.

Mrs. Clemens, not taking this view of the case, spoke at length through her tears.

'Well, sir, I suppose I ought to congratulate you; but I did not want so much for myself. Says I, " Betsy, one hundred is ample for me;" but I did not think she would have left my Mar— Mar—tha without a penny—no, not even a mourning-ring.'

'I assure you it was not from want of a reminder, Mrs. Clemens; for I waited, pen in hand, thinking that she would certainly mention her niece. At last I said, "Excuse me, madam, but have you thought of your niece?" "Man, who made thee a judge or a ruler over me?" was her answer; and she went on to say that my business was to write from dictation, not to dictate. So there was nothing more to be said.'

'My aunt was perfectly right to do what she pleased with her own money. I shall never complain, nor need others for me,' said Martha quietly.

She arose and left the room, and followed by the *atra cura* which ever pressed on her shoulders, she went into the garden of her aunt's house—or rather that of Mr. Marchbanks, for her mother was only a resident there on sufferance now. The weather was keen; and she took a shawl from the peg in the passage to the door leading to the garden, and went to strive in a quick walk under the cedars to escape from the anguish of continued uncertainty.

This hope to fly from thought in violent action always reminds me of the hurry of the unhappy hare in whose neck the weasel has fixed its teeth, and who hopes in flight to escape the agony which it carries along with it.

Martha, when she turned, saw Mr. Marchbanks coming towards her. Though she was irritated and provoked by his seeking her, she had accepted his chinchilla furs, and was bound to show him civility. 'Twas a mercy, she thought, she had not put them on that day; though she could hardly have explained the reason which gave birth to the feeling.

Mr. Marchbanks looked a very fine figure of a man as he walked up the avenue towards Martha. Forty years sat lightly on him; perhaps, too, the consciousness of great added wealth gave unusual buoyancy to his step, and elevated his head, and advanced his well-developed chest. He had the conviction, moreover, that he was going to give peace to a wounded spirit—wounded by her aunt's omission of her name from the will—by assuring her that Mrs. Carden had more than suspected his devotion to her niece, and had felt a conviction that the wealth would be shared by them for the rest of their united lives.

Martha tried for a set smile as he drew near her, and composed herself to listen as he walked by her side. He gave a nervous, 'Hem!' and began.

· 'I fear you may have been grieved at the disposition of the property left by your aunt's will, and may be disposed to consider her act ungracious, if not cruel, to you. Will you listen a moment, whilst I give you my interpretation of the matter? Your aunt was a lady of great penetration. Did she ever hint to you that I am—well, that my heart is engaged to any particular lady?'

Martha's face became crimson. She would not tell an untruth, and how could she . repeat what Mrs. Carden had said? She answered nothing.

'I am sure,' said Mr. Marchbanks, inspirited still more by her silence and her blushes, 'that she must have said that my dearest hope was to make you my wife.' And as he spoke he took her hand, and drew her arm within his.

Martha released her hand gently yet firmly, and drew a long breath. To the unfortunate hare with the weasel sucking her life-blood, the invitation to come and enjoy herself in the most delicious plantation of young peas would fall pointless. Had she never loved Philip, how better could she have been matched than with this well-favoured worthy man, of suitable age, and possessing wealth to which she could never have aspired, for it was the united riches of ' Carden and Marchbanks' ?

But her love for Philip had never slumbered or slept. It had become more intense as the day had passed since she had known he was in the neighbourhood and had not communicated with her. Now, when her heart yearned for some intercourse with him; when she longed with an insane desire to see him once more, to hear his voice even when addressing a stranger; when her memory represented him as she first saw him, tossed like a bundle of sea-weed to her feet, with large hollow eyes, pallid cheeks, and powerless limbs,—this stout healthy-looking man, with his ruddy face and broad smile, came asking her to be his wife! As if she could ever be faithless to Philip!

'I am sure, Mr. Marchbanks,' she said at length, 'I am very much obliged for the proposal, which is a very noble and generous one on your part, as I am utterly penniless. Do not think me ungrateful if I decline it.'

'Decline it!' cried the suitor, standing back for a moment, and gazing at Martha in astonishment. 'Do you mean to say that you won't have me?'

'I mean that I cannot accept your offer.'

'Have you quite made up your mind? Do not decide yet. Consult Mrs. Clemens. Do not treat me so unfairly as to say "no" without consideration.'

And Mr. Marchbanks looked grievously in-jured and a little indignant.

'It would be unfair indeed, dear Mr. March-banks, were I to keep you in suspense. Had I known you two years ago, the answer would have been different. Now it can be but "no."'

'Two years ago,' said the lover, with a tremu-lous quaver in his voice, 'my dear Mary was alive, and I wanted no love but hers.'

And his sense of injury became stronger as he thought of his Mary's devotion to him.

'I am very much grieved to have given you any uneasiness,' continued Martha gently; 'but I cannot help it.'

'You might help it if you liked,' said Mr. Marchbanks; 'and it is all nonsense to say you are very sorry, but can't help it. If you were sorry, you would help it.'

They drew near the house now, and Martha was glad to terminate the interview by leaving the garden and the rejected suitor at the same moment: she flushed and uncomfortable; and he flushed and angry—no man likes to be refused, and he went away greatly irritated against Mar-tha. At length, recalling every word she had ut-tered, he caught for the first time the meaning implied in the reference to the past two years. She meant to say that she would have accepted him, had she not had some previous entanglement or engagement. He stopped dead-short when this idea flashed on him, as if to welcome it.

'Poor girl! Probably she considers herself bound in honour to this other fellow. I daresay she had rather marry me.'

There was comfort in the thought. He considered the matter over composedly; and as the other man was not present, nor had been for two years, he had fair grounds of hope, he argued, that he should win the young lady ultimately; which was a comforting reflection, Martha having risen considerably in his opinion since her rejection of her suitor. Such value as we all attach to objects which seem above our reach!

He was not a man to loiter when work was to be done, and on the following day he took the will to town to obtain probate. Arriving late, he drove to the house of his brother, a solicitor in great practice; and to him Mr. Marchbanks not unnaturally showed it, saying that Sharpin had drawn it up, and he supposed it was 'all right.'

Mr. Marchbanks the elder looked grave on the subject, and said its validity might be disputed;

and proceeded to explain more than one blunder made by the framer of the document that might end in the overthrow of the will.

'Who are the next of kin?'

'A sister and niece are the only relations.'

'Ah, I see — Ann or Nancy Clemens. The other has nothing.'

'No. I think her aunt' — and then, withdrawing his purposed confidence, he changed the meaning of the sentence—'must have forgotten her. Do you think Sharpin intended to do me mischief?' continued the manager.

'I can't possibly say. He may have erred from ignorance, or he may think of working the next of kin against you — we don't know his motive; or he may be simply stupid, and in that case he will think it is all right, and take no steps at all. Is the legacy a large one?' he continued.

'*Very* large.'

'Then you could afford a slice to that niece to keep her quiet, as she seems not to have been benefited by her aunt's will.'

'She should be welcome to two slices, if she desired it,' said the manager, with a peculiar smile.

'What do you think of doing? Would it be better to see the ladies, and find out from their manner whether they have been talked to on the subject by Mr. Sharpin? I scarcely can believe that he would, or could very well, tell this of himself; but he might contrive to let them hear it mysteriously through the supposed revelations of his clerks.'

'Thank you, brother. My mind is made up as to what to do.'

And he shook his brother's hand, and left him.

CHAPTER XXVII.

'We of the offending side
Must keep aloof from street arbitraments.'
SHAKESPEARE.

THE next day Mr. Marchbanks called at an early hour at the Oak House. Some one left the sitting-room as he entered it, and he divined that Martha had done so, preferring not to see him after the last interview. Mrs. Clemens was seated at the table, which was covered by the skirt half cut out of a bombazeen dress, and various chippings of the material. A large pair of scissors, a needle-book, and reels of black cotton, with a roll of gray glazed calico, and one of crape, occupied the furniture about the room. Mrs. Clemens had evidently taken off her spectacles for the purpose of wiping away her tears. She arose when Mr. Marchbanks entered, and offered her hand to him with as much sweetness as cordiality.

'You will excuse this seeming litter, sir,' she said. 'Martha—' and here her voice quavered off into a sob,—'Martha, poor girl, said she would make up her own mourning and mine, to save expense.' And she wiped her eyes again.

'I think I have heard that Mrs. Carden had no relations but yourselves,' began Mr. Marchbanks.

'No; only Martha and me, poor dear!' said the sister.

Whether the 'poor dear' applied to the deceased or to the daughter, Mr. Marchbanks could not quite tell.

'I am afraid, madam, that I must appear to you in a most invidious position, as the possessor of the wealth you might naturally have expected to devolve on your daughter.'

'Well, sir, of course I should like Martha to have been remembered; but I can't say that I have any grudge against you for having so much. If she had but left Martha a hundred pounds, or even five pounds for a ring—'

'It was very extraordinary,' said Mr. Marchbanks. 'Have you any idea *why* Miss Clemens
was excluded from any benefit by her aunt's will?'
Mr. Marchbanks asked eagerly, being half fearful
of finding some flaw in the woman he wished to
marry, and thinking that she could not have in-
curred a punishment so severe without an adequate
cause.

'I cannot tell, except that she and Martha
disagreed about Catholics.'

'Ah-h!' said Mr. Marchbanks; 'she was always bitter against those Catholics.'

But he was happier in the thought that the
disagreement was on a point of doctrine, and not
of character.

'I hope I may have the pleasure of seeing Miss
Clemens. I believe she left the room as I came
in.'

'Yes. I don't know why she went away,' replied Mrs. Clemens innocently, to whom Martha
had said nothing of Mr. Marchbanks' proposal. 'I
will go and fetch her.'

'Pray do so, madam; I am anxious she should
hear a matter of business on which I have to
speak to both of you.'

Mrs. Clemens wiped her spectacles deliberately,

and placed them in their case; and going out, returned presently with Martha.

She came in, blushing awkwardly, and doubting whether to offer her hand. Mr. Marchbanks, not expecting it, made a low bow; then, seeing her hand half extended, he advanced his. But by that time Martha had withdrawn hers, and seeing this, he drew his back in haste, just as she was offering her own a second time, which, in his confusion, he did not take; and then they both sat down, with faces redder than usual, and Mr. Marchbanks 'hemmed,' and began his little speech.

'Ladies, I have, since I saw you last, shown my worthy friend's will to a lawyer; and he tells me that there are several points in the will which would give grounds for litigation, and which might overset its validity. As you ladies are the only relatives Mrs. Carden left, you would have the advantages of possessing the whole of this fine property should it be given against me. I will tell you honestly that the will is deposited in the Probate Court, and will pass probably unless a caveat is entered. I would advise you, then, to select any lawyer you please to be your representative in fighting this battle, if you desire to fight it. If you are willing, without litigation, to accept a compromise, you will not find me illiberal; but I tell you honestly, that'—and, honest man as he was, he spoke with an effort—'were I in your place, I should not compromise the matter, but fight it; for I think you will overthrow the will.'

'On what ground?' said Martha, now become very pale, but speaking very quietly.

'O, technical objections, very patent to lawyers, but perhaps not so much so to the uninitiated.'

'Do they mean to say,' said Martha, 'that my aunt did not intend to leave the money away from —from her own relations?'

'Well, no, not that exactly, Miss Clemens; I allude to the manner of leaving it. Some flaw in the wording may make the intention of the testator of no avail.'

Martha looked up inquiringly. 'Well, sir?' She was by no means quick at understanding a subject.

'It means, my dear,' said Mrs. Clemens, wishing to show Martha her own superior penetration —'it means, that this good gentleman thinks you have been hardly treated in this matter, and is willing to make it up to you as far as he can.'

'Nonsense, mother!' said Martha, with her face crimsoned with anger.—'Now, sir, I am slow at understanding these matters; will you kindly put me right, if I am wrong, as I state it?—My aunt expressed her wishes, or her will, as it is called, on this piece of paper or parchment. Her will was, besides the legacies to the servants and three hundred a year to my mother for her life, to leave all the residue of her property to you, and nothing to me.'

'Yes,' assented Mr. Marchbanks.

'In carrying out her intention, there seems to be some flaw by which her wishes may be contravened.'

'Yes,' again replied the manager; 'and I understand that you would have little trouble in overthrowing the will; and were you, ladies, my mother and sister' (a little gulp at this word), 'I should advise your trying it.'

'Dear heart!' cried Mrs. Clemens; 'to do such a thing as that—to go against poor Betsy's wishes, having seen her stretched out so in her bed of death, so helpless like—I should never go to sleep in peace so long as I lived!'

'Remember, madam,' said Mr. Marchbanks, 'that *you* are provided for by the will; Miss Clemens is not.'

He then turned to Martha, and said gently,

'What are your wishes, Miss Clemens? You have but to mention them, and I will cheerfully carry them out, whatever may be their nature.'

'It seems to me,' said Martha slowly, 'that if I saw my aunt dropping guineas into a bag which she had marked with your name, and there was a hole in it that she did not know of, out of which the money rolled, I should be a thief if I stood under the table and picked up the money never intended for me.'

'*In* course,' said the Cornish mother. 'Or if, in putting change into the gentleman's hand, some of it fell on the floor, anybody would be very dishonest who picked it up and walked off with it.'

'And, sir,' said Martha, 'it seems to me little short of an insult to come and offer to two females, whom you have no right to consider dishonest from anything you have known of them, money, which would be a reward for not stealing. You cannot alter my aunt's intention, which was to leave the property away from me, and to yourself. Unless that could be done, matters must remain as they are.

" What is done is done."

Neither my mother nor I could dispute the will, which *I* know for one to have been her desire, so far as excluding me was concerned. We thank you very much, for I am sure you mean kindly.'

'One word, my dear young lady. There could be no reproach applied to you by any one for trying this matter in a court of law, and you may be in consequence put into the possession of very considerable wealth. Excuse me, but your dear mother is no longer young, and her legacy is only an annuity. Surely you might try to obtain this property by law, and enjoy what the law gave you !'

'The law is blind,' said Martha. 'In this case, the Christian must be a law unto herself.'

She rose as she said this, unwilling to prolong the conversation.

'Then,' said Mr. Marchbanks, taking her reluctant hand, and in his eagerness utterly forgetting the presence of Mrs. Clemens, 'listen to me for a moment, my dear lady. There is not one person in ten thousand would have decided so nobly. They would at the best have fought for a liberal compromise on my part. Let me *give* you what, with this added wealth, I cannot require. Let me present you with ten thousand pounds, for which I can give you five per cent if you like to keep it in the firm of Carden and Marchbanks, or which you can place in the Funds. This would be far more agreeable to me than to know that I possess riches to which you would have been entitled had my dear kind friend been more tolerant.'

'You are very good and generous, Mr. Marchbanks, and if I do not say all I ought, it is not because I am not grateful to you, but that I never have many words to use, somehow. But, you see,' she added, 'that, first, I could not accept a gift from you or any person on whom I had not the claim of relationship; and, secondly, I should not like to take my aunt's money, which she did not wish me to have; and, thirdly, I do not think you have any right to dispose of her money in a way she would not approve, any more than you would to give it to a Catholic school for children, or to a convent of monks.'

Mr. Marchbanks looked at Martha with a glow of respectful admiration in his face and eyes, that made her modest looks seek the ground.

'A virtuous woman; her price is above rubies,' he thought. And gazing at the heavy features, now inspired by sentiments so noble, he felt even the attractions of the deceased Mary fade into misty images in the presence of the woman standing before him, who had refused to marry him three days before.

She left the room suddenly, and he had to recall the grief and mortification he had so recently felt, to prevent his following her into the hall, and renewing his entreaties that she would make him happy and set his conscience at rest by accepting him.

CHAPTER XXVIII.

'Fresh fields and pastures new.'

WHEN Philip had first arrived at Rome he felt himself suddenly divorced from all old and recent associations, and plunged into a new life, or rather,  into a higher phase of his former existence. It must be pardoned to my hero, that his first feeling, on contemplation of the Old Masters, was disappointment. There was a seeming absence of nature in the brown skins, the green skies, and the black backgrounds; but a little thought sufficed to prove to him that the skies had become green from repeated coverings of yellow varnish over blue; and that the madders, which had once been of the tint of life, had now come to resemble the colour of a mummy. But, underlying all these disparagements made by time, he learned to seek for, and to contemplate with an admiration mixed with awe, the wonderful conscientiousness with which the old painters had represented the human head and frame; the masterly force with which they gave roundness and solidity to their subjects; the tender touches with which they indicated the swell of the cheek, and the trying line leading from the nose to the mouth; until he began to revel in the truth, the power, the sweetness of their delineations.

His first feeling was akin to despair; and then he aroused himself to copy for his patron, with a mind overwhelmed by a sense of the beauty of what he strove to imitate. These efforts were no playwork. They occupied his every thought in waking, and many of his dreams. It was well that the gentle lady in whose house he resided, having heard that Lord Tynedale wished his protégé to learn English, insisted on making him name the different articles on the table at mealtimes. He gave a hurried and unwilling attention, and was glad to dart back to the painting-gallery to continue his labour. The athlete in a race thinks not, in the strain and tension on his body, of the hand that girded his loins or bound on his sandals, nor of the cup of water snatched from the friendly fountain to moisten his lips ere he started.

In the mental effort, aided by eye and hand, made by Philip, he had no time to think of the quiet convent where he had been reared, or of the friendly home and the kind women who had ministered to him in England.

Moreover he grew discontented with his progress; and this dissatisfaction urging him to obliterate and repaint his copy, gave the notion to the rest of the artists, and even to himself, that he was a bungler, and could do nothing.

All trivial fond records were swept away in the despair which deluged his mind as this conviction deepened on him. He saw other youths begin and finish their copies of the Old Masters, and take them away to sell them with much seeming self-satisfaction, and felt that he should have died with shame to have owned them as his work. His keen perception of what these copies ought to be stood in the way of his doing any at all.

At length, after many failures, he succeeded more to his satisfaction. His eye, by dint of constant attention to the original in all the different

hours of the day—in the cold morning light, in
the full revealings of the garish noon, and in the
mellow glow of sunset—began to appreciate more
fully the intention of the master. He began to
distinguish the delicate gray tint, though darkened by age and obscured by dirt, at the soft
edges of the shadows, to detect where the pink
madder had changed to brown, and to trace forms
nearly undistinguishable in backgrounds in which
green foliage had darkened into flatness.

At length he succeeded in making a beginning of the copy from Domenichino's Sibyl, which
satisfied him more than usual; and obtaining a
model as near as he could to the complexion of
the original, he made a study from life, with
drapery of the same texture and colour. Whilst
his copy of the original was drying, he began at
his lodgings his life-study, and worked on the two
canvases on alternate days. The Italian artists
looked at the progress of his picture with astonishment, and chattered like monkeys. To their
observations Philip was profoundly indifferent, understanding them but imperfectly.

The copy at length was finished,—the first-
fruits of Philip's labour and Lord Tynedale's com-
mission. A traveller, who had an eye for art,

saw Philip's study from the model at the house where Philip resided, and offered him twenty guineas for it. As Philip had not considered it worth the canvas on which it was painted, and had intended to paint over it, he accepted the offer gladly, and was inspirited by the circumstance. Evidently others thought better of his powers than he did himself.

The next copy he began was one of a Transfiguration, and at the same time he designed a picture which he intended as an altar-piece to the chapel of the monastery in which he had been educated.

The patron saint of his friendly monks was St. Anthony, and the subject which he chose was that of the temptation. He succeeded in representing the look of mingled terror and defiance in the head of the saint, as one of his hands grasped the sacred volume, and the other extended the cross towards the reptile brood emerging in slow progression from the depths of the cavern and circling round him; but when he came to the temptation most difficult to overcome, Philip's love of ethereal beauty made the female a failure. The creature he painted in a nimbus of light was the half-child, half-angel, whose image filled his memory as an ideal of beauty and of purity. The woman was not the impersonation of voluptuousness tempting to sin, but a glorified spirit, in the contemplation of whose loveliness St. Anthony might forget all mortal terrors, all human defilement.

He was very much pleased with his work, though his friends pointed out the failure as to the received notions of St. Anthony's temptation; and the English lady at whose house he resided said that, after the terrors of those evil spirits in their reptile form, an angel must have come and ministered unto him.

Was this angel to be the temptation of Philip's life?

CHAPTER XXIX.

'Plumed Conceit, himself surveying;
Folly with her shadow playing;
Purseproud, elbowing Insolence.'

GRAINGER.

. LORD TYNEDALE spent some weeks at Seadrift, and put up with the dulness for the sake of the improvement of his health. Perhaps the full-blown beauties and obliging manners of Mrs. Bolitho were not without their attractions, for his lordship liked the contemplation of handsome objects. At length he left Seadrift in some disgust. For some time he had been the monarch of all he surveyed. He was a lord, and in that titleless little locality he was regarded with.wonder and awe. Mrs. Bolitho, shrewd woman, got up several raffles on the strength of this lordworship; for his lordship always liked to draw for himself, and she found that the folks used to like to be able to say, 'I put into that raffle with Lord Tynedale;' or, 'I won that trinket at a raffle in which my Lord Tynedale adventured.'

At length his lordship's glories were partially eclipsed by a heavy gross body which intervened between his light and the admiring gaze of the Seadrifters. Mr. Mereside, recovering from his gout, and regaining his powers of locomotion, made himself exceedingly busy in the affairs of the town. Matters were shamefully misconducted; and he, instead of partaking of the soft undecided contemplative character of Hamlet, and crying,

'The time is out of joint ; O cursed spite,
That ever I was born to set it right !'

desired nothing better, with his active mind and

practical disposition, than to set everybody and everything right according to his own notions. He began to enjoy Seadrift;

'For man's neglect he loved it more.'

He looked at it with the kind of grim satisfaction with which an old woman, hired by the day to weed, regards the twitch-grass in the gravel, the thistles on the flower-beds, and the bind-weed smothering the gooseberries and currants. There was this difference between Mr. Mereside and the old woman—that whereas she would get paid for her work, Mr. Mereside, having in vain attempted to stir up the inhabitants to subscribe to the undertakings which he considered indispensable, and they but as the tithe of mint and anise and cummin, had himself to pay for the public works in which he chose to embark.

How the Seadrifters could sleep quiet in their beds with the parapet half washed away, he could not conjecture; he only knew that *he* could not. He declared that they were as lazy as the Spaniards; and told them that a friend of his with a companion, travelling in Spain, had come to the gates of a city after they were closed for the evening. No entreaties could obtain for them an entrance, and the result seemed inevitable that they must remain in the carriage for the rest of the night. At length the friend, who was a general, said, 'Twenty-two years since, I led my men in an attack on the north side of the city-wall, and breached it. A considerable aperture was made, through which the gun-carriages passed. Probably the wall has never been repaired; let us drive in that direction, and see.' They did so, and drove comfortably into the town.

Neither the scoffings nor the remonstrances of Mr. Mereside had any effect on the parochial pocket. The expense would be great. Mr. Mereside did not know how great it would be. 'It will be greater by and by,' he argued. 'Every winter there are tides which wash high enough to carry off the loose materials.'

Still he reasoned in vain.

Then he said, 'I will engage the men, and pay them myself.'

When the repairs were begun, Mr. Mereside was constantly on the spot, with his unaristocratic bearing and appearance, talking eagerly to the men, and directing their labour with more intelligence than was usual in the sleepy town of Seadrift. Nor would he consent to the smallest infraction of duty. With his large silver watch in his hand, he was out to see that they came at six o'clock to their work; and he was there again frequently in the course of the day to watch that there was no laggard in the gang of stonemasons.

By degrees this wealthy and energetic old man, who was willing to spend for the benefit of the town, began to extort the respect and gratitude of the many labourers he employed, and of those in a higher sphere who witnessed the expenditure of riches for the public good.

Lord Tynedale loathed the sight of the vulgar fellow, he said. His lordship was a moderate Whig, this man a vile Radical. Yet for all that, his lordship felt himself restricted to being worshipped by Mrs. Bolitho, and the small crowds collected in the library for the raffling. The library was in the lower room of the Queen of the East's residence.

Mr. Mereside, with a fiendish penetration, guessed my lord's foible, and determined to spoil his amusement and seduce his subjects from their allegiance. He went to the jeweller's, and bought ten pounds' worth of trinkets; and throwing them on the counter of the library just as the dice were about to be thrown, whilst his lordship, cold and stately, was looking on, and being looked on with reverent eyes, he cried,

'There! raffle for these, if you care for such trifles. You are welcome.'

'This fellow is fit only for a bear-garden,' muttered his lordship.

He felt himself eclipsed by this vulgar parvenu, who purchased popularity by lavishing his wealth on others, whilst my lord was obliged to be content with the lesser degree of admiration he excited for spending it on himself.

There was something pugnacious and impertinent in the little turned-up nose and sparkling black eyes of Mr. Mereside. He seemed a not inapt representative of the middle class of the people—clever, energetic, and unpolished, withal a smart man, as the Americans would say, and one who, without being dishonest, would take every advantage in a business transaction.

My lord, with his watery blue eyes rather projecting from his face—a fact of which he was very proud, as he declared that it was a mark of fine breeding in all animals, including mankind—with his profile so well cut, and pale, and thin, that his head looked like a cameo from the antique enlarged to life-size, with his slender figure and his dignified carriage, his feeble resolution and his high sense of honour—seemed a representative of the aristocracy.

Lord Tynedale paid Mrs. Bolitho next morning, and left Seadrift, notwithstanding the tears that stood in the eyes of the buxom Queen of the East. I am not sure that their resemblance to those of the parvenu in colour and brightness did not make his lordship contemplate the possessor of those beauties with a feeling of repugnance.

CHAPTER XXX.

'Ah, who can tell how hard it is to climb
The steep where Fame's proud temple shines afar ?'
BEATTIE.

LORD TYNEDALE turned his back on Seadrift; and returning to his house in Park-lane, summoned his young relative from the country, and announced his intention of going immediately to Rome.

'That young painting-fellow,' he said, 'must want looking after. He has been there now considerably longer than I at first intended. I should like to see how he is getting on.'

'But, uncle,' suggested the girl, 'it seems to me that he has always been asking for orders; and that it cannot be his fault that he is still there, if you have given him none to return.'

'Well, he will probably get them now *vivâ voce*,' replied her relative; 'so you will be ready to start to-morrow.'

It was Lord Tynedale's order, that in return for the liberal allowance made to the young lady for clothes, pocket-money, and lady's-maid, she should be prepared to go any distance with the old peer at a moment's notice. So the order did not take her by surprise. They travelled by easy stages, for it was his lordship's care never to fatigue himself unnecessarily; and six weeks after found themselves in a grand and somewhat dreary palace in Rome, Lord Tynedale having sent on a courier to one of his English acquaintances residing there, and desired him to hire a suitable residence, in a room of which the young painter had been directed to place his copies, that his lordship might criticise them at his leisure, without the restriction which the presence of the artist might occasion; for Lord Tynedale's sense of politeness generally restrained the expression of an adverse opinion at first; it was only 'while he mused' that 'the fire kindled, and at last he spake with tongue,' and with a warmth of vituperation that reduced the unfortunate victim to meta-phorical cinders under his wrath.

The day after the arrival of the travellers, Geniveve rose early; and in exploring the stately rooms of the palace, entered the one which contained the recently-painted pictures, and remained transfixed with admiration of their freshness and their pure yet mellow tone. Philip had placed them in the light which he had considered best adapted for revealing what excellences they possessed; and the young lady, who knew something of the difficulties of art (not yet overcome by herself), was enchanted by the results of Philip's labours.

A small copy of Raphael's celebrated picture of the Assumption of the Virgin was placed in a handsome gold frame on an old carved arm-chair with a back of faded crimson velvet.

Geniveve knelt down to admire it more closely; and was so captivated by the beauty of the upturned face of the angel, that after having admired the other copies, she returned to this one again and again.

After looking at it some time, the love of imitation grew strong within her; and she went for her sketch-book to make a study of it. It did not look difficult; but when she began to form the outline of the upturned face, it would not look like Philip's copy. She procured some bread, effaced the outline, and recommenced it. It would not do. Mortified and angry with herself, she tried again more carefully, flinging back the intrusive curls that fell over her eyes and on the cheeks flushed with eagerness and the sense of failure.

In the mean time the hour had arrived appointed by Lord Tynedale for Philip's visit; but his lordship, not feeling himself in force after his journey, declined to leave his room till the evening. Philip was ushered into the saloon where his paintings had been placed. It was so large, that though his name was announced by the servant, Geniveve, occupied by the trouble of her outline, heard nothing, and kneeling with her back partly turned to the entrance from the anteroom, saw nothing.

Philip looked on the golden wealth of flowing hair, the graceful turn of the neck and shoulder, and the sweep of the drapery extended on the floor; and he drank-in draughts of such delight as painters taste when they gaze on beauty which inspires their genius and taunts them with the impossibility of representing it.

It was a picture in itself; and the scene of its

loveliness so filled his senses for the moment, that
he enjoyed it without thinking who the vision
might be. It was not till she half turned her
head to pick up a bit of bread she had dropped,
that the downcast face, more visible than it had
previously been, showed him that it was the original of the picture which he had copied twice, and
had admired to the point of almost worshipping.

He scarcely knew what to do; he felt like a
thief, standing there and looking at the unconscious
sketcher, who was obliterating some lines and re-
touching others, utterly ignorant of his proximity.

After remaining in contemplation of the fair
young creature for a few minutes, his eyes fell on
her work; and the instinct of the artist broke the
spell of his silence.

'The line of the left eye is too high,' he said in
Italian. 'It is not in the proper curve; it is out
of drawing.'

She turned herself suddenly, still on her knees,
in astonishment and anger at the criticism, and
met the eyes of an exceedingly handsome young
man—tall, slight, and dark, though with a broader
chest than when he was shipwrecked at Seadrift.

'You think me very impertinent?' he said
humbly.

'O, no, not at all; but people never like to be told they are wrong at first. Are you—the—Mr. Philip Rose?'

'If you are angry with my criticism, you may soon have your vengeance'—he meant revenge, but could not think of the right word in English—'when milord examines my copies.'

'I am sure *you* need not fear criticism, your copies are so very perfect.'

'Ah, you have not seen the originals.'

'Pardon me, I am familiar with each and all of them. I am an old traveller, and resided here for many months with my uncle when I was much younger than I am now.' This was said with all the dignity of seventeen.

There was a little pause; and Geniveve did not raise her eyes, for she felt that the painter was taking a mental inventory of her face. She blushed under the scrutiny; and to throw off the awkwardness she was beginning to suffer from, she meekly offered her begun sketch to her companion, and said that, as he had told her that it was wrong, he was certainly bound to show how the defect might be rectified.

Philip knelt down to rest the sketching-block on the chair by the back of which the painting was supported; and Geniveve innocently knelt by his side to watch his correction of her drawing.

To his mind and with his Catholic ideas the picture of the Virgin and Child seemed a shrine, the velvet-covered chair the altar, before which Geniveve and himself were prostrated in the prayers of the same faith.

He was troubled, however, by her proximity. Her fair hair brushed against his cheek; and when she turned to ask him a question, her fresh rosebud lips were very close to his paler ones.

'How your hand shakes!' said Geniveve, with a little astonishment that one who drew so well should be nervous.

Philip could not rise easily whilst she knelt so near him, and did not like to request her to move. She, turning over in her mind why he should be nervous, thought he was dreading the interview with Lord Tynedale. She forgot her eagerness to watch his drawing in this new aspect of the matter; and rising, she went into the antechamber to order an attendant to inquire if Lord Tynedale would like some of the smaller paintings to be taken to his lordship's bedroom, and to inform him that Mr. Rose was awaiting Lord Tynedale's commands.

The agitation of Philip, however, had not proceeded from terror of his patron. He felt self-assured as to his own powers now; and having suggested several pictures to copy, by letter, to his lordship, and executed all that Lord Tynedale had seemed desirous to possess, Philip had painted some original pictures, for which he had obtained a good price from some English and Russian travellers, and had transmitted the money to that convent in the mountains of Spain where his youth had been spent, in gratitude for the monks' care of him. He felt convinced that his copies were good, and dreaded no adverse criticism, which he knew would be ill-founded.

A message came from Lord Tynedale's room to express his regret that he was unable to receive Mr. Rose that day, but added that he hoped to be sufficiently recovered to see him on the morrow at the same time. Meanwhile James was to transport one or two of the smaller copies to his lordship's room.

'Then I should take my leave,' said Philip, bowing profoundly to the young girl.

'Stop,' she cried; and turning to James, who was lifting the painting of the Virgin and Child to take it away, she said: 'James, come back as soon as you can, and tell us how my uncle likes it.'

' Yes, miss.'

And Philip understood the quick perception of what she believed to be his anxiety, and her desire to alleviate it.

There was a short interval of silence after the servant's departure; then, turning her lovely face towards her companion, she said:

' If my uncle likes your works, he will be enthusiastic in their praises. Any fault he may have to find will only come with a reaction some days after; but I do not think there will be any decrease of his admiration in the present case, as it must be so well-founded.'

James came back shortly to his young mistress.

' My lord is quite delighted with the painting, miss. He has had it placed where he can see it conveniently from his bed, and has sent me for another.'

Philip, thinking he had no longer any excuse for remaining, bowed himself out. At the entrance of the antechamber he turned for one more look, and saw the charming figure of the girl in her pure white drapery, with the light striking from the high narrow window on the golden glory of her hair, and the angelic expression of her face; and he returned to his temporary home with a sense of suffocating depression in his breast; for he felt that he loved the fair creature so much above him with that one passion of a man's life, by the side of which all others seem dwarfed; and he knew, moreover, that he was pledged to the woman he had left in England, to whom he was bound both in honour and gratitude — gratitude for unbounded tenderness, and even for the preservation of his life; honour, because he had given his word that she should be his wife.

CHAPTER XXXI.

' Some voice whisper'd o'er me as the threshold I cross'd,
" There is ruin before thee ; if thou lovest, thou art lost." '
MOORE.

LORD TYNEDALE came out of his room after luncheon, and went with Geniveve for a drive. He was full of praises of the work executed by the young Spaniard, in which his young relative joined. It had been their custom when in Italy before to take Geniveve's sketching-block, and make studies of any picturesque fragments of columns or luxuriant and graceful foliage. Lord Tynedale observed that Geniveve was removing the outer sheet of the block; and seeing the head of the angel, he detected at once that there was a bolder and more decided touch of the pencil in parts of the sketch than could have emanated from the uncertain manipulation of his niece.

'This is very good,' he said.

'Yes, uncle. I did not do it properly, and Mr. Rose corrected it. I wish he would give me some lessons.'

'Why not?' cried the peer defiantly. 'Confound it! I suppose I pay him for his time, and he must do just what I please.'

'You are very good, uncle; but I thought you might object to the loss of his time in teaching me, when he might work for you with results so much more satisfactory. May I ask him tomorrow?'

'Ask him? Certainly not. I shall order him to give you an hour's instruction every day. Name your own time.'

In the following forenoon, Lord Tynedale saw the rest of the copies, of which he greatly approved, and suggested to Philip that he wished him to give lessons in painting to his young relative. Philip flushed crimson, and looked so disconcerted, that his lordship might have been forgiven for the impression that the artist considered it below his dignity to be a drawing-master.

Philip suggested that such an arrangement would seriously interfere with the prosecution of any great work Lord Tynedale might wish him to undertake; that he had never been in the habit of teaching, and was by no means sure of being able to communicate what he knew. He was trying to find some other excuse to make, when he was warned to desist by the fury sparkling in the light-blue eyes of the peer.

'Confound it, sir!' cried Lord Tynedale, 'do you mean to say that you object to give lessons to *my* relative?'

Geniveve entered the room by a door toward which the peer's back was turned, and hearing tones of anger, she looked pleadingly and reproachfully at Philip.

'I should have been an obedient pupil, Mr. Rose,' she said, 'and done all in my power to profit by your instructions; but as you object, I could not now accept your teaching, were you willing to overcome your dislike to the office of master.'

The young Spaniard looked down. Certainly, judging by the misery displayed in his countenance, virtue was not its own reward. From a sense of duty he had given up an occupation for which he longed as the traveller over arid sands desires a draught of clear cold water, and he had displeased his patron and vexed the creature on whom he doated.

The peer looked haughty and angry, and was silent; Philip was depressed, and said nothing; and Geniveve turned the conversation, with a desperate effort of politeness, to some subjects unconnected with painting. She was always forgetting that Philip was a Catholic, and now began to speak of the miraculous liquefaction of the blood of St. Januarius, which had just taken place in the church of S. Gennaro at Naples, and which she had witnessed a year before. She began to question how the miracle was accomplished, then stopped suddenly, thinking that she was treading on unsafe ground. Lord Tynedale was still silent, for he was too much of a gentleman not to have felt disturbed by the fact that the artist had been subjected to the expression of his wrath.

Philip, who was, though a good Catholic, rather incredulous as to miracles being worked in the present day, felt awkward and uncomfortable when that subject also was touched on. He shrank from the ridicule expressed by heretics for sacred things, yet he could not defend the extravagant pretensions of his Church.

So he floundered about to avoid any conversation on the miracle, and said that if he had objected to teaching Miss Geniveve, it was from the fear that he might be delayed in any other copy Lord Tynedale might desire; of course his lordship's wishes were laws to him. Lord Tynedale was placated; but Geniveve sharply and decidedly declared that she had always thought she should like to become a pupil of Signor Bellizzi, whose style she much admired; so she would not trouble Mr. Rose for any lessons. Then with a slight bow she left the room, and went into the gardens that lay at the back of the palace.

Philip asked if his lordship had any more commands for him, and on receiving a negative was about to depart, when Lord Tynedale sent him to find James, as he wanted an arm to support him to his room. Philip offered his own, and deposited the peer on his sofa; then he left him, having first secured the attendance of the valet on his lordship. As he was returning, he looked out on the gardens, flickered with sunshine and shadow, rich in autumnal flowers, and melodious with the splashing of fountains. Foreign gardens, with their cypress depths of shadow, and their graceful statues gleaming against the dull tint of those pyramidal evergreens, possess beauties borrowed from their climate in which our ornamental grounds are deficient.

Philip longed to make his peace with the young lady, but he knew not how. If he saw her again, perhaps some opportunity might arise of saying something to diminish her displeasure. He yielded to the temptation to follow and seek for her, trusting to chance to aid him. A sudden turn in one of the stately walks showed her to his eager eyes seated on the stone border of a fountain, over the edge of which she was leaning. She seemed thoughtful, and was unconsciously scattering the petals of the roses of which her lap was full on the surface of the water. The spray of the fountain fell sometimes in a shower on her head, a circumstance of which she seemed unconscious or careless. She looked like a wood-nymph making her toilet in that natural mirror.

'How beautiful she is!' said Philip; and his hand sought his sketch-book, in which he began to represent the unconscious girl. 'Ah, if she would but remain as she is one moment longer— one knee drawn up on the old gray-stone brim, the other foot just touching the turf, and her downcast face smiling at the loveliness of its own reflection in the water—what a charming picture I could make!' thought Philip.

The sunshine flickered over her hair, and the shoulders covered with her white dress, leaving the sweet face in half shadow.

She remained sufficiently long for Philip's practised pencil to convey her resemblance to paper slightly, but with sufficient hints as to his future treatment of the picture he hoped to make from his study; then he retired comforted, without having addressed a word to her in mitigation of her displeasure. His love for his art, and some vague hope that if he succeeded in making an attractive picture from his sketch she might forgive him, gave his mind a pleasant object of occupation.

The next day Philip called again at the palace; but Lord Tynedale was indisposed, and could not or would not see him. He was ushered into a room, where the young lady was seated before a large fragment of a bust called Morna, with a gigantic portfolio supporting her drawing-paper raised on an easel, under the direction of an eager gesticulating Italian drawing-master.

She turned and bowed slightly to the Spaniard, saying,

'I fear my uncle is not well enough to receive you; and I regret that the time Signor Bellizzi can give me is so valuable,—as you, Mr. Rose, feel with regard to your own,' she said meaningly, —'that I cannot attend to you myself.'

Philip, flushed with vexation, bowed, withdrew, and went back to his studio with a deep feeling of mortification. When in the course of the day he saw Lord Tynedale's carriage drive by with his lordship in it, and his niece by his side, Philip returned to the gardens to make studies of the fountain, and of the autumn flowers that dipped into its brim, and made warm tremulous tints in the troubled waters.

'O, that I could get her foot!' he said; and as the next best thing he went to the palace, and by a few compliments to the looks and a small sacrifice to the cupidity of her maid, obtained from her the loan of one of the tiny slippers Geniveve was in the habit of wearing.

'I will return it to-morrow,' he said.

Geniveve's vexation had driven her to take lessons from a man whose paintings she had professed to admire, but about whose work she did not really care. She had this mortification as a punishment—that showing one of Philip's copies to her master, he burst into raptures at its excellence, and declared at once that it must be the performance of the young Spaniard, as no Italian copyist could equal him in skill.

When at the end of a week Philip, by incessant work, had finished his picture of Geniveve, in obtaining the likeness of which the copies he had formerly made of her portrait really conduced, he carried it with a silk handkerchief over its surface to the palace, and placed it on a chair in the light most likely to do justice to its beauties. No one was in the room. He loved his work; he thought it a charming picture, both in the principal figure and in the accessories. He seated himself opposite to it, to admire it at his leisure, and then thought that a few more touches might improve it. 'Twas too late now, however; he heard a step, and the stately old lord appeared leaning on the shoulder of his beautiful niece. Philip, seated between two windows, was nearly obscured by their heavy damask curtains, and sat, with eager eyes and senses all alert, to hear judgment passed on his performance.

'O, uncle!' cried Genieve, seeing it first.

'By Jove!' cried the peer, 'that is you; a great deal too pretty, though.'

'O, uncle, is it not beautiful!' and she blushed up to the roots of her golden hair, tinting with pink the delicate blue veins.

CHAPTER XXXII.

'A jealous man wishes himself a kind of deity to the person he loves. He would be the only employment of her thoughts.'
ADDISON.

PHILIP was as happy as a painter can be. The poet whose heart felt flame when first he sang to Beauty's ear never felt the ecstatic delight of the young painter who has fitly represented the form of the woman he loves, and has heard her approbation unconsciously expressed.

Lord Tynedale had that 'instinctive grasp of oaths,' and 'the passion for filling them into the crevices of common speech,' so universal amongst old men fifty years since.

'D—n it,' said the peer, 'he is good enough to paint *me!*'

Lord Tynedale could think of no greater privilege by granting which he could more fitly express his admiration of the artist.

Genieve heard and shuddered—not at the oath ; those little condiments, with which old gentlemen belonging to the bygone period warmed up their conversation, meaning nothing by them, she was too much accustomed to hear to regard in any way—but at the notion of the terrible punishment in store for Philip, which outran the offence he had committed against her by fifty degrees at least.

The peer drew a chair up to the picture, and sat down to admire it at his leisure.

'He knows how to paint a foot—and a shoe,' he added.

'The shoe is marvellous, so like mine!' said Genieve. 'I wonder how he came to paint me in that position. I don't remember having sat upon the stone-work of the fountain.'

'''Tis a fancy sketch no doubt, with an accidental likeness to you.'

'I know 'tis my shoe, from the buckle on it.'

'Yet—no, 'tis you yourself! Did you sit to him?' he said with a sudden suspicion that he had been deceived, turning round the inquiry of his blue projecting vacant-looking eyes on her.

'Sat to him without your lordship's permission!' said the girl; 'I am astonished that you can imagine such a thing!' And the beautiful young face gleamed anger back on the old peer with looks as proud as his own.

'Well,' said Lord Tynedale, 'I'm glad he has painted this picture for me. I remember now that he copied the portrait of you which I gave your father, and he has probably got a good deal of help from it in obtaining the likeness.'

Philip sat in nervous awkwardness, neither attempting to conceal nor reveal himself. He was sorry to have done what might seem dishonourable if he were discovered; for he had accidentally escaped being seen at first, and then had afterwards felt too shy to come forward. He was greatly relieved when the peer rose slowly, and again supporting himself on the shoulder of Geniveve, passed out into the garden.

When they had departed, Philip left his retreat and followed them slowly. As he turned the angle of the garden-walk he saw them stop; whilst from the movement of Lord Tynedale's arm, he saw the peer was speaking to his niece of the execution of the accessories, of which he was observing the originals.

He longed to join them and receive their com-
mendations, to fight his painting-battles over
again, and show them where he got that fragment
of stone, and those flowing tresses of graceful
climbing-plants, that turf of vivid green turning to
gold in the sunshine, and those clusters of crimson
roses fringed with their brown-and-yellow autumn-
tinted leaves. But he remembered his position,
and that the hired painter had no right to intrude
himself unsummoned on the society of the proud
peer and his young relative; so he returned home
with the listless feeling of an artist who has
finished one picture and not begun another, and
also with a parent-like yearning for the last offspring.

So Philip strolled about over Rome, and tried
to think of its glorious past, to admire its picturesque ruins, and to 'find a fane in every sacred
grove,' in which he worshipped the Egeria of his
thoughts.

He thought he might call next day without
being considered intrusive; but next day seemed
to be put off to an incalculable distance.

'If she would but forgive me,' he repeated to
himself, 'I should not care if I never saw her
again.' Thus does love deceive itself.

CHAPTER XXXIII.

'Seest thou a man wise in his own conceit, there is more hope
  of a fool than of him.'   *Prov.*

THE next day came at length. When Philip
awoke, and before full consciousness dawned on
him, he fancied he heard the voice of Geniveve
crying out, 'O, how beautiful!' and he lay still,
smiling with closed eyes, lest the vision should
fade. When Reason returned, with her cruel cold
definiteness of rule, line, and measure, there was
still enough to make him happy in the remembrance of yesterday.

Pride goeth before a fall, is the proverb. Ela-
tion always, in this world of ups and downs, seems
to precede mortification.

When Philip called to receive his patron's commands next day, he was shown into the room in
which Lord Tynedale was seated, with a pile of
English newspapers by his side, which he, spectacles on nose, read with great seeming interest.
In the recess of one of the large windows he saw
projecting a fold of white muslin, and knew that
it was the skirt of Geniveve's dress. He went
up to Lord Tynedale, who rose politely and bowed

to him, and then reseating himself, and returned
to the article that interested him.

'I called, my lord, to ask if you have any
orders to give me as to what I am to paint.'

Philip had a hope that he should receive a
compliment on the picture he had left on the chair
for inspection; but that which seemed so all-im-
portant to the painter had passed from the mind
of the peer. He had forgotten that he had ever
seen it; so he looked up with a little irritation
of voice at being disturbed, and said that he was
busy then, and would attend to him presently.

Philip bowed, and walked towards the window;
but when he drew near it he stopped, for he heard
the sweet voice of Geniveve talking to some one,
to which the answer seemed to be a short affected
laugh.

His footsteps made her look round; and she
saw him, and turning to a light-complexioned
young man standing near her, she said, with the
instinct and habit of good breeding,

'Lord Lemesureur, permit me to introduce
to you Mr. Rose.'

Philip flushed consciously to himself, and
loathed himself for being so contemptible as to
be influenced by the sound of a title. Titles were

plentiful as blackberries abroad; but he knew the value of the English peerage, and though he had never felt humiliated by the rank of his patron, but rather the reverse, the juxtaposition of the two names, Lord Lemesureur and Mr. Rose, uttered by the lips of the woman he dared to love, affected him with a feeling akin to mortification.

Geniveve looked at him and wondered why he blushed, but considered he looked handsomer for the flush on his cheek. Lord Lemesureur looked haughtily and indifferently out of his light hazel eyes, just bent his head slightly in acknowledgment of the introduction, and turned to resume his conversation with the young lady. In politeness she could not but answer, and Philip found himself in the way.

He had been temporarily dismissed by Lord Tynedale, but desired to wait; then he had gone to address the young lady, and had felt he should have been better absent altogether.

He turned away and wandered about the room. The only picture in the saloon was his own, still resting on the chair where he had placed it. He heard a low laugh proceeding from the window, and in his irritable sensitiveness fancied that the pair were amusing themselves at his evident

admiration of his own performance. This deepened the colour afresh on his cheek. How he
hated that young man, and felt more than half
inclined to extend the feeling to the young peer's
companion! He was disposed to leave the house
and return again the next day; but the remembrance of the listless hours of aimless sloth
he had passed in the interval between his two
last visits, and the recollection that he was bound
to wait Lord Tynedale's pleasure, kept him, though
unwillingly, in the room.

Geniveve was too well-bred not to know what
was due to any one, however low born, who had
the manners of a gentleman. She walked up to
him, followed reluctantly by the young peer.

'O Mr. Rose,' she said, blushing, 'I am so
charmed with that picture! It was very good of
you to give my uncle a surprise so agreeable. We
can never thank you sufficiently.'

Lord Lemesureur had dragged his slow steps
after the lady. He minced his words as if he
disdained them—as if they were dirty, and he had
to go over them on the tip of his tongue. Each
came out distinctly in a small voice, which was
innocent of the slightest manly intonation.

'A very creditable effort!' he said, with a self-satisfied smile. 'Really now, considering the difficulty of the subject, for which we feel disposed to make every allowance, you have not painted it badly at all.'

Philip would have liked to have stabbed him. Foreigners do not long to plant their fists at the root of their adversary's nasal organ, as is the fashion with us islanders. I am sorry that Philip, brought up in a monastery of monks, knew nothing of 'the box.' Lord Lemesureur, on the contrary, looked at him with a complacent simper, expecting him to be grateful for the amount of commendation he had lavished.

Geniveve felt diffident and abashed at the idea of praising any portion of the figure or drapery ; but, more sensitive than her noble companion, she wished to wipe out the mortification she was certain he must feel, so she said,

'How skilfully you have rendered the bit of ivy creeping between the disjointed stones of the fountain ! How prettily it clasps the masonry, as if seeking for the moisture contained within it ! You must have painted that from nature.'

'I painted it from a drawing made on the spot.'

''Tis a pity, when your performance is really so very creditable for a beginner, that you don't pay more attention to aerial perspective. That distance should be lost in mist;' and his lordship stood back, and half closed his cattish - looking eyes, which ran up from the nose, with eyebrows following the same direction.

'I paint what I see to the best of my power,' said Philip shortly, in English, with a slight accent, and speaking with great deliberation. 'No doubt, with the benefit of your lordship's instruction, who would seem to be so good a judge, I should execute a painting more worthy of yours and of this lady's attention.'

He spoke with a sneer, which Lord Lemesureur was too conceited and obtuse to perceive, though it was patent to Geniveve, who coloured with vexation.

The young peer, encouraged by what he considered to be the teachable mind of the painter, went on.

'Yes,' minced he, 'I *do* know a little about it, and I shall be very happy to give you a few hints while I remain here. The fact is, I never learnt painting; but I have an intuitive knowledge, on most subjects, of what things ought to be. Now that hand resting on the stone is quite out of drawing, and not nearly white enough for Miss

Tynedale's. I think, if I were in your place, I should get my brush and paint it out at once.'

'Anything else, my lord?'

'The foot is better—easier to execute, being covered with the shoe; but the leg drawn up on the stone-work is very clumsy, and not properly fore-shortened. Ah, I was always considered a good judge! Mr. Lawrence told me that I was the best judge of a cravat he ever met, and that the hints I gave him were invaluable:'

'So invaluable,' replied Philip, 'that I will not do your lordship the injustice to deprive you of any more of them, and will leave to this lady the undisturbed enjoyment which she must receive from hearing them, as she is also devoted to art.'

Thus saying, with a face white with passion, he returned to Lord Tynedale too impetuous to remember his politeness.

'The morning is slipping away, my lord; and my time, which belongs to your lordship, is valuable for that reason. Have you any commands for me?'

. 'No—yes. Ah, that is a charming picture you have made of my niece—exceedingly clever. I would not part with it on any account. I want a copy of it for a friend of hers in England; also, I want a copy of St. Stephen by Francia in the Borghese Palace. This will occupy you some time.'

'Which shall I undertake first, my lord?'

'The St. Stephen. You can copy the portrait for me at any time. If you return to England with me, perhaps I may sit to you myself. Do you think you could do me justice?' said his lordship, rising to show a manly front, but leaning his hand on the back of his chair to conceal his feebleness.

'With a subject so dignified, I should think I could scarcely fail, my lord.'

The peer smiled weakly, and Philip bowed and took his leave.

'Unfortunate that I am,' said the painter, 'I have contrived to get into trouble with both the lady and that accursed fool the young peer. I hope they may not influence the old man against me.'

CHAPTER XXXIV.

'So have I seen, in black and white,
A prating thing, a magpie hight,
    Majestically stalk—
A stately worthless animal,
That plies the tongue and wags the tail,
    All bluster, pride, and talk.'

                                    GRANVILLE.

'I HAVE work before me,' said Philip. 'I am a fool ever to have been ruffled by such a conceited prig of a man. How can Miss Tynedale tolerate such a shallow creature—a man who has weakness written in every movement of his face? 'Tis a fine thing to be a lord, certainly. Every word the creature utters is gilded by the silly fellow's title. He is listened to by men and adored by women by reason of his birth. How can she suffer him?'

Then he began to think what she might have done to express her dislike to his society, had she indeed felt any. Reason told him that she had only acted with common courtesy to both young men. She had tried to compliment Philip, and had left her place near the window with thoughtful politeness, to lead the conversation in a direction in which he could join. She was not

answerable for the weak impertinences of her companion.   She had looked vexed and annoyed at
Philip's vexation.   Then a flood of tenderness
rushed over his feelings, and tears came to his
eyes.

He could never seek to win a creature so superior to himself.   What weakness of character to
think of her at all !   He would cease to do so; he
would demolish the sketches he had made—first
from the portrait copied in England, then the
studies he had made for the picture at the fountain.   He opened his portfolio to collect these, and
came on a picture of Martha made roughly, as a
study of the one he had afterwards sold to Lord
Tynedale.   He turned from the unconscious image with loathing, and with the feeling which
prompted Bertram to say when he saw Helena in
the distance,

'Here comes my clog.'

Had he not weakly engaged himself to that woman, he would have been free to win the love of
this heavenly creature.

'Free !' he laughed scornfully; 'free to win !
free to spring from the earth, and clutch the bright
radiance of the moon !'

He, a poor painter; she, a descendant from a

long line of ancestors, and the heiress of great personal wealth and unencumbered landed property! Truly, his chance of succeeding would have been great! and he laughed himself to scorn again.

He gave way to the impulse of the moment, and taking his penknife out, he cut the canvas of Martha's picture into strips, and took up his sketch-book to destroy the studies of Geniveve. But he could not.

' No,' he said; 'I'll keep them for the present. She has not yet been desecrated in my imagination by a marriage with that nonentity dignified by a title. The sketches are my own. There is the delicate curve of the mouth, the rounded chin, the soft blue eyes, and flowing hair.' He kissed the slight image frantically; and then, inconstant as the winds, he sat down to paint—not the copy ordered by Lord Tynedale of the martyrdom of St. Stephen, but another likeness of Geniveve in a different position, which should be, he resolved, even a more correct resemblance than the one by the fountain. He stopped for an instant, and laughed.

' I am like Fabricio Nunez,' said he, ' who swore that he would abjure poetry, and sat down to write a farewell to the Muses.'

He worked incessantly for three days. He knew 'every line and trick of that sweet favour.' Geniveve had a rival in her own image; for the young painter loved his work. Still he longed to see her again, to watch if he had equalled her inimitable beauty. St. Stephen was forgotten till Philip was told by the servant that the valet of my lord wanted to see him.

James had been sent by Lord Tynedale to ask why the copy of the St. Stephen had not been begun. His lordship and the young lady had been at the Borghese Palace on the former day to see how far he had progressed, and found several artists at their work, but Mr. Rose was not amongst them. Philip had been pale enough from his seclusion, and now became still paler; so that James inquired respectfully if he were ill.

He took the hint, and assigned it as an excuse gladly, saying he had not been well for the last few days—indeed ever since he had last been at his lordship's palace. He would call at once on Lord Tynedale, and make his apology for seeming neglect of his orders. James thought it would be best. The valet felt a little pity for the poor young man, exposed as he knew he would become to all the varieties of his lordship's temper.

Philip thought little of his apology. 'I shall see her again,' alone possessed his mind.

It took some time for Philip to make himself fit to appear; especially as a bladder of Prussian blue had burst from too impatient manipulation, and had sunk under his nails. This delayed him; and though he left his palette loaded with paint, and his brushes dirty, it was some time before he was dressed and had arrived at the palace.

James had delivered his apology, and made his peace with his lordship, who inquired so politely after the health of the young painter, that Philip blushed at the untruth of his excuse, thinking too what an aggravation of his fault it would have appeared had Lord Tynedale known how his time had been spent.

'I am so sorry you have been ill, Mr. Rose,' said the soft tones of Geniveve; and Philip, looking up, caught the pitying expression of those speaking eyes.

They were at luncheon; and Lord Lemesureur was of the party.

'Have some?—sit down!' said my lord in a tone of command.

Three plates only had been set; but James,

who waited, placed a fourth, with a knife and fork for Philip, and then was dismissed to his own dinner by his master.

Philip had received an almost imperceptible recognition from Lord Lemesureur, which he returned even yet more distantly. The blood of an old guerrilla chief flowed in his veins; and gentlemen of his nation are not deficient in haughtiness.

Lord Tynedale's teeth were false, and a slight attack of paralysis made deglutition an anxious process; so he never talked whilst the serious business of eating was to be performed. Some boiled chickens, a tongue, an omelette, and some fruit composed the luncheon. The chickens were carved by Lord Lemesureur, who helped Lord Tynedale and Geniveve; and without inquiring whether Philip would eat any, he remained with the knife and fork suspended, whilst he gave an animated account to Lord Tynedale of some red deer which he had sent to his lordship's park in Norfolk, and of the difficulties which had attended their being transported thither without injury. Geniveve grew impatient, believing the neglect to arise from contempt of the painter, and said,

'I will thank you to carve some chicken for Mr. Rose, Lord Lemesureur.—Will you allow me to cut for you a slice of tongue?' she added, addressing Philip also.

'I take neither, I thank you.'

He would have liked some, but wished to show that the omission did not affect him. Philip's lips were parched, and his tongue was dry from anger.

'A peach, then?' said Geniveve.

'Thank you, yes.'

There were but three, for it was late in the season, and they were scarce.

'A peach is my favourite fruit,' said Lord Lemesureur, looking up with some anxiety from the half-consumed plateful of chicken to which he had helped himself.

'Indeed!' cried Geniveve indifferently, selecting with careful precision the finest, and placing it on Philip's plate.

Philip looked up with a glow of grateful feeling in his dark face.

Lord Lemesureur saw the look, and was more indignant than jealous. He had considered it a piece of presumption in that painting-fellow, as he called Philip in his own mind, to make a portrait of his patron's relative without permission, though he had presented it to Lord Tynedale. He thought it was taking a liberty to represent the features of the future Lady Lemesureur without having been called on to do so; and he considered that it was quite derogatory to Lord Tynedale's dignity and that of his young cousin, that the painter should be invited to take luncheon with them.

Then, to prevent Philip's joining in any conversation, he began,

'But, as I was saying to you before this—a—gentleman arrived, about Almack's. When you are introduced, which I suppose will be next year, I will use my influence with my aunt, who is one of the lady patronesses, to get you into her set.'

'You are very good, but I don't think I am particularly desirous of going to Almack's. Should I be so, I have no doubt my uncle could do all that is necessary.'

'Ah, my dear Miss Geniveve—pardon me—nothing but the simplicity of sweet seventeen could excuse that impression. You have no idea of the difficulties of getting invitations; and unless you mix in a certain set, neither rank, beauty, nor breeding can give you the words of fire which can thaw those frozen circles. I can assure you I saw the sweetest girl—the daughter of a Suffolk country gentleman—who had a partner, and stood up·in a quadrille then forming. We looked at

them, poor innocents, for an instant, and then left
them standing, and moved off to a different part
of the room. They were not of our clique. 'Twas
the greatest fun 1 ever saw—capital!' And the
young peer gave a little foolish laugh.

'D—d bad manners!' murmured Lord Tynedale.

'Is it possible,' said Philip, 'that an English
peer can be proud of an act of such ill-breeding,
exercised on a young and beautiful girl?'

'Pray, Mr. Rose, who are you?'

'A Spaniard, sir!' shouted Philip; 'and never
before did I feel so rejoiced that I am not an
Englishman and a peer.'

Now this was ill-bred and injudicious on the
part of Philip; for one of the peers present had
done him kindness, and conferred on him benefits;
but in his blind wrath, in his thoughts there was
but one peer in the world. Lord Tynedale—who
belonged to an age when, with all its debauchery,
there had been a more chivalrous devotion to women than was possessed by the set in which Lord
Lemesureur mixed—felt all his honest sympathies
go with Philip's wrath, and was not in the least
irritated by this sweeping reproach to the English
peerage. He was sorry, however, for the ruffling

between the young men. In the first place, it
increased the difficulty of deglutition by rendering
him nervous, and then disturbed the digestion of
what he had already swallowed. He made a silent
resolution, that he would never again admit any
one at luncheon-time. A bit got the wrong way,
and he was seized with a fit of coughing and choking, which made Geniveve nervous, and alarmed
both young men into silence and partial forget-
fulness of their mutual dislike. When the old
peer recovered, and by the aid of a glass of sherry
succeeded in getting rid of the obstruction in his
throat, Philip was filled with penitence for his own
ill-breeding.

'I beg your pardon, Lord Lemesureur, for the
intemperate expression of my opinion just now.'

Had he stopped there it had been well; but he
continued,

'You have an English maxim which says that
the truth should not be spoken at all times.'

Lord Lemesureur looked at the speaker vacant-
ly, as if he had meant to convey, Did this fellow
speak? Then he turned his head towards Geniveve, and addressed her on subjects in which it
was impossible for Philip to join: of the hope
his elder sister had expressed that Geniveve would

go and stay with her on her return to England; of the house she had recently taken at King's Lynn in Norfolk; and of the new governess she had engaged for her little girls.

Lord Lemesureur had chosen topics from which he knew Philip must be excluded; but he would have rejoiced to the extent of his feeble powers of receiving pleasure, had he known the shock which those words, 'King's Lynn,' last uttered by Martha in his presence, conveyed to the Spaniard. Since Philip had left Seadrift, he had mixed in refined society. The gentleman and lady at whose house he resided were persons both well-born and well-bred, though not wealthy enough to dispense with a quiet inmate like Philip when such could be found.

The few words of English he had uttered on his arrival made them rejoice that his studies in that language had not proceeded farther. The intonation, they said, was *very* vulgar and provincial, and he had connected these criticisms with the remembrance of Martha and her mother. He would have thought of them tenderly notwithstanding, and still remembered the benevolent shrivelled old face, that had ever looked kindly on him, with affection; but the knowledge that he was bound in honour to marry a woman whom his new acquaintances had unconsciously pronounced to be vulgar made his spirits sink, especially when his ear, made more observant by these criticisms in his new language, told him how perfectly pure was the grammar, pronunciation, and tone of Geniveve's conversation. Even Lord Lemesureur, affected and mincing in his words, was free from any taint of vulgarity. He talked weak nonsense ; but the words defied criticism, though meaning there was but little in the sentences he strung together. So Philip winced at the name of King's Lynn in Norfolk, where he knew Martha and her mother had intended to go, and where probably they were still residing.

It was doubtless very wrong in Philip first to engage himself to Martha, then to fall in love with a picture of another woman, and finally with the original of the portrait. But he was very young, and the circumstances under which he had been placed were peculiar.

So whilst Martha was giving up the chance of a fine fortune for his sake, he was chafing at the weight of the chain which bound him to her. Two years had nearly elapsed, he told himself, since they parted (it was really a year and eight months). Not the slightest communication had passed between them during that period.

He had learnt both to speak English and to write it with tolerable fluency; but he had carefully abstained from writing to Martha. He felt like a traveller in the Alps, who dares not speak, lest the avalanche loosened by the sound should fall and crush him.

———

CHAPTER XXXV.

' But gnawing Jealousy, out of their sight
Sitting alone, his bitter lips did bite.'
SPENSER.

WHEN Lord Tynedale rose from the luncheon-table, he asked for the support of Philip's arm to his bedroom. James had not probably finished his dinner, and he could command the services of the young man whom he supported by his patronage.

When Philip had performed this duty he had no excuse for prolonging his stay, though he yearned to go back and see if Lord Lemesureur were still with Geniveve.

There were hours of daylight yet sufficient to

begin his St. Stephen, and he went to his work with a heavy heart. He had been set at naught by that foolish young nobleman, had lost his temper, and felt bound to apologise. The only slight gleam of comfort arose from the look of tender pity he had received from Geniveve when he had first seen her. That she had given him the best peach he was unconscious; so much had the young peer's omission to help him disturbed his equanimity, that he had not perceived the preference. Her interference with regard to the plate he ascribed to her politeness.

'What idleness,' he exclaimed, tossing back his dark curls from his forehead, 'to think of her at all! I *will not!*'

And he went into his painting-room, and saw something in the lovely face on the canvas which he fancied might be improved; took up his palette and maul-stick, and seating himself before the picture, never stirred till the departing sun refused longer to aid him by its beams.

'Never mind; 'twas a broken day. To-morrow I will certainly attack the Francia. Perhaps they will come again to see how I make progress.'

He worked well when he had once begun. There is a birdlime in every picture to a painter thoroughly imbued with love for his art, which glues him to its surface till he is satisfied that he shall succeed. He took no note of time whilst he worked on his copy. He had a less clear idea of Geniveve's face as he painted on the countenance which, caught by heavenly glory, seemed as the face of an angel. No man can be thoroughly unhappy who has health and an occupation in which he delights. Grief may crush for a time, and uncertainty as to his fate may relax the muscles of the painter's weakened arms; but an abstract love of art is a wonderful tonic to the mind, and consequently to the body. As he progressed, he lost the expectation of seeing Geniveve and Lord Tynedale, till he had gone on nearly to the completion of his copy.

Copying an ancient master has a wonderful power of making the artist live again in the life which expended itself two hundred years before, and left traces of its genius, its industry, of its aspirations, and of the brilliant success that crowned them. With admiration for the artist increasing every hour as the eye took note of each bit of drapery flowing gracefully, and each accessory skilfully filling its appointed place, each tint of colour cunningly contrasted with its opposite,

was mixed profound respect for the concentra-
tion of mind which could disregard every temptation to swerve from the great end in view—
success.

Philip was pleased with his work, and received
the compliments of the artists who painted by his
side.   With this encouragement, yielded with the
enthusiasm of their southern temperament, he felt
he could endure the fatuity of Lord Lemesureur's
criticisms.   One day as he had descended from
the platform on which he had painted, and was
making some smiling observation to one of his
fellow painters, he heard a voice which made him
start, and turning, he saw Geniveve leaning on
the arm of Lord Tynedale.

His lordship could not find terms sufficiently
laudatory to express his admiration of Philip's
performance.   It was the finest copy he ever
saw.   'Twas as good as the original.   'D—n it!
'twas better than the original!   Rose, come and
dine with me to-day.   I dine early, being an invalid.   Perhaps during the evening you might
catch an idea or two of the best position for a
painting of me; it will require all your thought.'

Philip bowed, and expressed his gratitude for
the invitation, and his willingness to give all the

efforts of his mind to painting a portrait of his lordship.

He went, and to his intense relief the incubus in the shape of Lord Lemesureur was not present. He enjoyed some conversation with Geniveve during the dinner; his lordship, being too much occupied in eating, cared neither to lead nor to join in it. Geniveve did her part with the tranquillity of a young lady accustomed to the duties of society, and possessed by a conviction that she could not be found wanting either in their knowledge or their practice.

Lord Tynedale sat in a great arm-chair, and after finishing his dinner, when the dessert was placed on the table, he took an extra glass of sherry, and shortly after fell back asleep. The young people dropped their voices respectfully whilst they ate their fruit; but tired of the compulsory tone of the conversation, Geniveve, looking out on the gardens through the windows, which opened on to them with folding-doors, and seeing them aglow with a rich red sunset, asked Philip if he would walk, as the air seemed genial, and it would be agreeable to exchange the atmosphere of the dining-room for that of an autumn evening.

It could not be doubted that Philip assented

gladly; and drawing a light shawl over her shoulders, she led the way with stealthy steps lest she should awaken her relative.

> ' See you tread softly, that the blind mole
>   Hear not your footfall,'

said Geniveve, smiling; but she added, 'I ought to apologise for quoting Shakespeare to a foreigner, and one who stated his pride in not being an Englishman,' she added slyly.

'Ah, you should forget my sins, when I expressed my penitence so meekly to that gentleman —no, to that lord.'

'Your distinction is somewhat bitter; but I admit that you had great provocation,' replied Geniveve.

They walked on in silence for some time; when the perfume of the flowers and their tangled tracery of pendent blossoms, warmed and illuminated by the last rays of the setting sun, impressed the frame of Geniveve with a vague feeling of delight, and she exclaimed,

'How beautiful!'

'I was just feeling that,' said Philip, regarding her with eyes that pointed the compliment.

He, poor fellow, meant it in good earnest; but it was received as a matter of course by Geniveve.

That young lady was perfectly free from all jealousy of other women, and was also perfectly sweet-tempered, for the best of reasons—her delicate beauty was so supreme that she could fear no rival; and with wealth, health, rank, and the observance which follows in the train of those bright realities, the world was to her a vast pleasure-ground, of which she seemed to be mistress. Had any one told Geniveve she had a ring on her finger, or a bracelet on her arm, she would have thought the observation superfluous. Thus, when Philip implied that he thought her beautiful, she only smiled, and gave a little inclination of her head, as if she thanked the politeness intended.

They walked on till they turned the corner and came to the fountain, the falling waters of which now caught the cloud hues of the setting sun, and fell like showers of topazes, sapphires, amethysts, and emeralds.

They stood still for a few moments in quiet enjoyment of the loveliness of nature, and then the lively brain of Geniveve sought for information on a subject that interested her. Turning to her grave companion, whose dark and thoughtful profile showed clearly against the evening sky, she put a leading question.

'Do painters paint from what they see, or what they imagine?   As my maid would phrase it, do they paint pictures "out of their heads"?'

'No good painter does — no man who ever wishes to be a successful painter; for without truth as a foundation of rock, paintings are like those houses built on sand, of which my kind lady at the house read to me from her English Bible.'

'Then the picture you painted of me at the fountain cannot be a good one.'

'Pardon me,' said Philip; 'it is as good as my talents and industry could accomplish.'

He felt hurt at the reflection on his performance.

'Because you had no model to draw it from,' she added, looking at him inquiringly.

'I sketched it from yourself,' said Philip, slowly and guiltily.

'No; I am sure you could not have done so. I never gave you an opportunity.'

'You have a poet called Pope who says,

"Snatch ere she fade, the Cynthia of the minute."

That is what I did.'

'But how?' asked Geniveve, with a little flush

on her cheeks. (No one likes the idea of being watched unconsciously.)

'Pardon me,' said Philip, seeing the flush and detecting a little tone of vexation in the young lady's voice; 'I will explain.'

'Then,' said Geniveve, 'as we cannot place chairs as they do on the stage, when two persons are about to impart anything to each other secretly, so that all the audience might hear, let us sit on the edge of the fountain in default of a better support.'

Philip did not like this exordium. It was too light and mocking, in his opinion, for a subject so deep in its interest to himself; but he spoke after a little pause.

'I must entreat you to hear me indulgently, if I took too great a liberty in sketching you when you were ignorant of my proximity; but on the morning when Lord Tynedale did me the favour to propose that I should give you lessons, and I had the misfortune to displease you by declining that honour, I was so very wretched, that I followed you into the garden to try to make my peace; and seeing you in a position so graceful—such a nymph-like image of youth and beauty—I made a study of your position in my sketch-

book, which afterwards expanded into the painting which I placed in the saloon for your
uncle's inspection. Of the accessories I made
separate studies, when you and Lord Tynedale
went out. So you see, Miss Tynedale, I did
my best as an artist,' he added, with a faint
smile.

Geniveve was silent for a few moments, and
then, looking up in his face with a timidity which
made her doubly charming, she said hesitat-
ingly,

'Do you think me very stupid about drawing?
Did that faulty line in the angel's head stamp me
as being utterly unteachable?'

Geniveve knew that she was a beautiful young
lady, but was very doubtful of her artistic talents.

Philip looked at her without answering for a
few moments, and then said,

'I do not consider you at all unteachable. I
think you very clever; and painting is only a
torrent of natural talent rushing constantly in one
direction.'

'Then why did you mortify me so by refusing
to teach me?'

Philip's brow grew darker, and he made no
answer.

'Speak! answer me!' cried the imperious beauty.

'Pardon me, Miss Tynedale, I cannot answer you truthfully, and it does not accord with my notions to tell an untruth. Pardon me that I can neither satisfy your curiosity, nor that I could give way to your wishes when Lord Tynedale expressed them.'

'But,' insisted Genivève, 'you retracted your refusal, and said you would give me lessons.'

'That is true,' said Philip. 'It only proves my weakness. I am very grateful you declined to profit by my tardy repentance. 'Tis better as it is.'

CHAPTER XXXVI.

'Try to imprison the resistless wind,
  So swift is love, so hard to be confined.'
                                        DRYDEN.

GENIVÈVE could not understand, for she had been unaccustomed to opposition. All her masters had seemed delighted by her acuteness and proficiency, and this young Spaniard, though he appeared to admit her beauty, evidently distrusted her talent. She knew she was lovely, but her

conviction that she had a facility in learning drawing was a matter of doubt to her own mind. She
could sing like a seraph, for a fine and flexible
voice made singing come as it were by nature.
Dancing also had seemed intuitive; and some of
her poetical efforts had been pronounced to be
charming—for her fine ear had made it easy to her
to use the words at her command harmoniously
and to lisp in numbers, for the numbers came.
But painting was essentially an art that required
application and labour; it necessitated a greater
knowledge of proportion and perspective than she
had or was likely to acquire. Painting is a jealous
Muse, and insists on reigning supreme; otherwise, she flies off to votaries who are more assiduous
and constant. She requires to be worshipped from
the first dawning of light till the eyelids of her
disciples droop from weariness into sleep.

A young lady about to be introduced into
society was not likely to be thus devoted to art.
Nevertheless, she resented Philip's objection to
teach her, and distrusted his silence as to his reasons for declining to do so.

'Then,' she said, after a pause, 'you do think
me stupid, after all?'

'I assure you,' he said gravely, 'that is not

my reason. I do not think you otherwise than clever. But is it fair, young lady, to press a man for his reasons, when he is unwilling to render them?'

'So, besides being averse from teaching me, you try to prove that I am ill-bred,' said Geniveve.

'Pray don't misinterpret me — you have so much the advantage of me in facility of expression. Perhaps if you knew Spanish, we should understand each other better; but in English I feel much like a "dumb dog," incapable of barking with any appreciable result.'

'But, after all, your meaning is sufficiently evident, that you do not care to convey to me any portion of your knowledge of art.'

Philip was silent, and Geniveve leaned over the fountain, and dipped her hand into the water.

'How bright the skin looks,' she said, 'under the surface!'

And the inside of her fingers, with their rosy tint, looked like the inside of a pink shell.

'Look, your shawl is dipping in the water; it is not fit for you to wear now. Allow me to go to the house and ask your maid for another.'

'No,' said Geniveve, wringing the moisture

from the fringe; ''tis of no consequence. We will both return to the house. My uncle will be awake by this time probably, and ready for his coffee.'

As they drew near the palace, Geniveve stopped, and cried:

'O, my ring! I have lost it!'

And they retraced their steps, looking on the ground.

'Is it of value?'

'O no, of no value at all; only 'tis stupid to lose anything, however trifling.'

'I fear you will not find it now—'tis too dark,' said Philip. 'Besides, I think it probable that when you shook the water-drops from your hands, after wringing the shawl, it dropped into the fountain. Did you value it?'

'No, not particularly. I bought it myself, and a very few pounds will replace it. I even doubt whether I should care to offer a reward to one of the gardeners to pick it out of the water. Some of the pearls had become discoloured; it was not worth anything. But we *must* go in now. My uncle will be impatient.'

'Miss Tynedale,' said his lordship, when they opened the window, 'I have waited for you.'

This was a crushing reproof, but not the truth;

for Lord Tynedale had drank his coffee very deliberately under James's administration. Philip
thought that he would be nervous lest his niece
should suffer from the effects of the night air, not
knowing the character of the peer sufficiently to
be aware that he was nervous about no one but
himself. Like Louis XIV., no one had a right
but himself to delicate health. He claimed a
monopoly of all illnesses.

'I am very sorry I am late, uncle,' said Geniveve cheerily; 'but I lost my ring, and went
back to look for it.'

'Did you find it?' growled the peer.

'No, uncle.'

'Glad of it,' said he; ''twas a d—d ugly thing.
Hope I shall never see it again.'

'Very likely, uncle. I think, as you rejoice
so over my misfortunes, you are bound to replace
it with a prettier one.'

'Umph!' said my lord. 'Your allowance is a
liberal one, young lady.'

'Think of the sentiment, uncle. Your gifts
are always so valuable to me.'

'Yes, so they are; or the jewellers tell a pack
of lies, and are arrant cheats. Come, give us
some music.'

'Old or new, uncle? German or Italian?'

'Neither. Sing, "As I walked forth in Bedlam." That fellow Moore has put a pack of words to it that I don't care a curse about; they possess none of the tenderness of "The Maid of Bedlam." You may swear when a poet comes to tagging his verses with a simile, that the feeling that prompted their composition is unreal. An Irishman's notions of liberty are license and the power of robbing his richer neighbours, and his heart "indignant breaks" when he finds the law too strong for him.'

'Uncle, I'm ashamed of you. You a Whig too! An immoderate Whig you should be called.'

She ran to her harp, and sang to her accompaniment on its chords, 'Awa', Whigs, awa'!' to her uncle's unbounded delight, and Philip's wonderment at the fine quality of her powerful voice and at its skilful management.

This last was not extraordinary, for the years she had previously spent in Italy had been devoted to the cultivation of her musical talents, and her beautiful and flexible voice had excited the enthusiasm of the masters by whom her studies had been conducted.

Remembering her uncle's request, she sang

'The Maid of Bedlam' with exquisite pathos; and
when she came to the lines—

> ' Her chain she rattled on her arm,
>   And sweetly thus sang she :
> " I love my love, because I know
>   My love loves me" '—

some recollections of the past started tears in the
eyes of the old man. Then she sang to him ' The
Rose-tree in full bearing,' the words of which he
preferred to Moore's ' I'd mourn the hopes that
leave me.'

' Ah,' he said thoughtfully, ' that song was
sung to me fifty years ago.'

Fifty years seemed to him not a very long
time; it had soon slipped over. To Geniveve
and Philip—one seventeen and the other twenty-
two—it seemed some incomprehensible ' unknown
quantity.'

' I am going to bed now,' he said, wiping his
eyes. ' Rose, give me your arm to my room. Miss
Tynedale may sing you one of her fine Italian
squallings when I am gone, if you like such.'

When Philip returned to the room, he stood
a moment at the door gazing on the beautiful
creature who was seated at her harp, and just dis-
tinguishable through the strings. Then, advanc-

ing towards her, he claimed the promise Lord Tynedale had made in the name of his young relative; and Geniveve sang, without any delay or affectation, with finished skill, ' Una voce poco fa,' as she had been taught to execute that charming melody by Madame Camporesi.

Philip was entranced as the liquid notes were warbled out with the precision of a musical-box. There is something catching in singing; the hearer longs to join in it. As she turned idly over the leaves of the book, Philip saw the ' Buona notte amata bene,' and murmured the air. Geniveve asked him to sing it, and he complied immediately in a rich sonorous voice; on which, and on the expression with which he rendered the words, Geniveve complimented him. Then another turning of the leaves revealed that charming old French duet, ' Reposons nous ici tout deux,' which they sang together with mutual satisfaction; when Geniveve, remembering that it was getting late, rose with a slight blush, and held out her hand to bid Philip good-night. She did it because she was an English girl, and had felt the intimacy grow up suddenly between them in their concord of sweet sounds. His sallow complexion flushed, as, with the reverence and devotion of a foreigner to his patron saint, he took the small pink-tipped fingers in his slightly-formed hand and pressed his lips on them. The first impulse on her part was to withdraw her hand; the remembrance of his foreign extraction prevented the incivility, and she bowed and said, 'Buona notte,' repeating the title of the song he had just sung. The touch of her hand thrilled through the sensitive frame of the unhappy young man, who stood before her spell-bound with the intoxication of the moment, carried to excess by her quotation of the words of the song. His quick remembrance supplied the remainder of the words; and thence sprang the mad thought, which scarcely amounted to a hope, as to whether she could have meant to apply the rest of them to him.

END OF VOL. II.

ROBSON AND SONS, PRINTERS, PANCRAS ROAD, N.W.

www.ingramcontent.com/pod-product-compliance
Lightning Source LLC
Chambersburg PA
CBHW021841070726
47496CB00022B/1496